T0146985

23
DIFFERENT
JOBS

Daniela Loria-Caschera

23 DIFFERENT JOBS

iUniverse books may be ordered through booksellers or by contacting:

iUniverse
1663 Liberty Drive
Bloomington, IN 47403
www.iuniverse.com
1-800-Authors (1-800-288-4677)

Because of the dynamic nature of the Internet, any web addresses or links contained in this book may have changed since publication and may no longer be valid. The views expressed in this work are solely those of the author and do not necessarily reflect the views of the publisher, and the publisher hereby disclaims any responsibility for them.

Any people depicted in stock imagery provided by Getty Images are models, and such images are being used for illustrative purposes only. Certain stock imagery © Getty Images.

ISBN: 978-1-5320-7473-8 (sc)
ISBN: 978-1-5320-7474-5 (e)

Library of Congress Control Number: 2019906455

Print information available on the last page.

iUniverse rev. date: 08/14/2019

This book is for everyone who pursued
their dreams part-time.

Table of Contents

ALIENS

At my old job I had to use my own laptop. I spent about 60 percent of my time browsing through dafont.com and downloading fonts onto Microsoft Word. This was only sort of my job, as I worked for a prominent blog (that I won't mention) as one of four graphic designers, and we sometimes needed new fonts for titles or body paragraphs in posts. I also had to make ads for videos we would release. I always needed fonts. This was all a waste of time because what I was doing was picking fonts I might need later, only to browse through dafont.com, again, whenever I needed a font.

I would also dabble in coding—I was consistently working on a game where all the little trinkets on my coworkers' desks interacted. Lucille, who sat beside me, had a wooden crab that completely came apart—she got it in Cuba and said the wooden sculptures were like that so people could pack them easier—and if I clicked it, it would crab walk over to this 8-bit Darth Vader bear (inspired by the one Marc had on his desk a couple cubes down) and cut its head off. I didn't really know what else crabs could do. That was pretty much what my day-to-day looked like, sometimes busier, sometimes slow, but ultimately? I worked a regular job, had a regular life, and never really did much worth noting.

I know you probably think that I was sort of a loser, and you would be correct. I was sort of just in a rut, you know? I had goals and aspirations, but they all fell to the wayside at some point.

Now I'll explain what actually happened because that's the most interesting part of the story and what the Historical Society wants me to write about. I felt like it was important to explain a little bit about myself before the actual story—for some context—so hopefully any future readers aren't too bored by this point. Keep reading as this next part will probably have an answer to one of your assignment questions.

Everyone kind of knows the circumstances around the events of the Day. First the sirens, then some sort of speaking, and everyone thinking it was just happening in only their heads but really everyone could hear the same thing. That was a weird feeling. I remember really hoping no one could hear my thoughts and that this was just some sort of weird dream. I sometimes passed out in the quiet room at work, and though I couldn't remember going to the quiet room, I assumed I was asleep.

Everyone stopped on a dime the moment we started hearing words in a language that felt otherworldly. I could feel when words ended and began but I couldn't really connect them to anything, like how if you know French you can pick up Italian or Spanish words here and there.

I remember a high-pitched whine, like mic interference, and then suddenly words started sounding like English, which I thought was interesting. I wondered if people who spoke other languages heard different languages. Then I started registering what the disembodied voice was saying.

So, they played the first message, which was something like, "We have reason to believe your planet will be responsible for a universal catastrophe, and as a result, we have decided to launch a full investigation. Since you ignored our countless attempts to inform you of your trial, we have graciously brought the courtroom to you", and I remember being in a state of disbelief, thinking that maybe it was just our office managers playing a trick on the workers, as they have been known to do because they're 'hip', but then the 9/11 Monument was arbitrarily destroyed.

The aliens continued their speech, and proclaimed, "We have decided that the person who will represent you will be Katie Vega." I suppose these aliens had never encountered a planet with people who had the same names, because they were sincerely taken aback when I yelled, "Which Katie Vega? There's more than one!" after they announced the name of the Representative Elect. There was a small amount of sputtering on the alien side of the broadcast, and the voice changed from a neutral, slightly off-putting voice to a shriller, almost comical one, that reminded me of Rick Moranis and Kermit the Frog mixed together. That only made it feel more like a dream because why would anyone but me mix those two voices together?

"Wh—Which Katie Vega? You mean there's more than one? Why would there be more than one?" I got the feeling this voice was not used to interacting with those who lived on the planets they were going to destroy.

"Well, I knew at least two Katie Vegas growing up, and I'm sure if you searched 'Katie Vega' on Facebook—"

"Facebook? Is that that thing where you make a profile and you can search for your friends and put links to funny videos on their walls?" The Ruler seemed genuinely interested. I found this comment strange because it seemed to know a little about Earth culture, but, again, did not know that people sometimes had the same name. Astounding.

"Yes, it is. But anyway, search 'Katie Vega' on there and—"

"Very well. Are you a Katie Vega?" Everyone listening could tell that the Ruler and its cronies were clearly discussing in their alien language exactly what course of action to take. They were murmuring like politicians at a McDonalds, as my mother liked to say, which I think means something like *politicians don't talk shop in public places.* My mother was a hippie.

"I can't believe these are the aliens we get stuck with. What's your technology like up there? Are you even translating this into the languages of Earth, or do you legitimately speak English? Is this from a fucking novel? Is there a fish I should have in my ear?" I was particularly proud of that reference because I didn't encounter many people who had read any Douglas Adams books, so I thought it was rather clever. I wracked my brain to find out which Sci-Fi novel from my youth I had encountered recently that would illicit this dream; none seemed quite right.

"Young lady, we will destroy another monument to prove our power!" I remember mouthing 'young lady' in disbelief.

"Let's say that I am a Katie Vega. What am I supposed to be doing? And I'm speaking in strict hypotheticals here, I may or may not be a Katie Vega."

"Well, Katie Vega is the person who will make the case regarding the Earth's importance in the history of the galaxy. It was all in the speech, did you not listen at all?"

Before I could respond, the Ruler said, "Aha! You are Katie Vega. Our computers just told us so." It sounded so childish it almost made me laugh. It seemed as though the computers had not really told them what my name was, and they were just pretending; I mean, I seemed to be the only one speaking, so it didn't matter what my name was.

"Okay, so I am Katie Vega. Now I'm supposed to give some sort of speech about why the Earth should be saved?" I sat down in my chair and thought that, since this was a dream, I could definitely smoke a bowl at my desk and not get in trouble, and even if I got in trouble it wouldn't matter because it was a dream. So, I pulled my pipe and grinder out of my little hidden purse compartment and proceeded to smoke. I thought it would help me to make a lot of good statements about the Earth. The aliens gave an exasperated sigh and said that Yes, I was the one who was supposed to explain the Earth's value.

"What value? I mean, we haven't explored enough planets for our culture to have really pushed itself into the consciousness of others. To Earthlings Earth is important, but to other planets, Earth is probably just a blue marble, right?" I inhaled and felt myself sink a little into the chair. I usually picked up my weed from a co-worker, but he hadn't been able to grab for weeks so I had grabbed from a drug dealer friend of a friend. She was nice, but her weed was only mediocre. I think she got it about a week old and not properly stored from a dispensary.

"Well, what about humans? Aren't you going to say how amazing humans are even with all their flaws and they deserve to live?" I could tell that it truly was a haughty old alien who was not used to people talking back to it; you know, being insubordinate.

"Well, can I ask you a question first? Why is Earth even on the list of planets to destroy if you think we have too much culture... et cetera?" I couldn't figure out how to end that sentence, so I ended it with 'et cetera'—you know, what anyone does when they want to seem intelligent. You'll probably use this in your essay.

"It's just part of our job, ma'am. We don't make the rules; we just follow the ones set out by the Federation." I heard what sounded like papers shuffling, which was weird, because I didn't think aliens would need papers. I noticed that this voice was a little deeper and more authoritative than the first voice, the voice of the Ruler, and that made me question the integrity of this destruction plan. I finished my second bowl and dumped the ashes from my pipe onto the floor of my cubicle, putting my pipe and grinder in a Ziploc bag I found in my purse, and then it hit me.

"Wait, you work for The Federation? Are you saying Roddenberry was right? Do you work for fucking Star Fleet?" There were many moments when I was sure this could be nothing but a dream, and this was one of them. Did I mention I thought this whole thing was a dream? I cannot stress this enough. I mean, wouldn't you?

"Dear human. We are simply doing our jobs and would request that you, insert na– Katie Vega? Is her name Katie Vega, guys? Okay—Katie Vega, proceed to make your case for why your planet should not be destroyed." This was a different voice, and this alien was obviously reading from some sort of Mad Lib-type template thing, which has a name, but I can't quite recall what it is.

It was at this point I decided to put some effort into my dream and say what I was thinking. "Why shouldn't Earth be destroyed? Who says it shouldn't—who says it *shouldn't* be destroyed? Maybe humans deserve to be eradicated from the universe," I walked out of my cubicle and went around to Lucille's, picking up her wooden crab. "Humans are like that guy you dated in college—or girl, or whomever, I shouldn't assume anyone's preference—who was so perfect when you were just getting to know him or her or them. They were good in bed, nice to look at, into all the cool music that you didn't even know existed, they were into sports just enough to be fit but not a pompous jock. But then, about three weeks after you go on your first date, they start showing their true colors, and you remember what you heard from the other girls in your college about them. At first, it's just harmless flirting, and you do it, too, hoping they'll get jealous, but they don't. They just go and fuck another girl who falls in love with them too quickly, just like you. They're still all those remarkable things, because they were always honest, but so many bad things, too, because they were just as insecure as you were, just, a—selfish prick, but better looking." I walked around a little more, and I felt that the aliens were hanging on my every word. I didn't think I was really speaking well, and my thought process was convoluted, but I knew what I wanted to say, and I was floored at having an audience.

"Humans don't change. We post pictures and videos online and force everyone to be part of our lives, but we only show them the best parts when life is just shit. When people don't answer our texts, we get upset, we take away their privacy... For every video someone shares on Facebook from the Make-A-Wish foundation, there are hundreds of thousands of other instances we don't see on video of warlords forcing cocaine into the wounds of young children to get them addicted enough that they'll do anything to get their fix. In 1915 we have the Armenian genocide, from 1939 to 1946 we have the Holocaust, and before that the Turks enslaved the Greeks for 300 years—and not to mention race relations in America for the last, what, 500 years? Countless other things I can't even remember hearing about which are just vile. We don't even have secure enough science to know how exactly *how* cruel our ancestors were. Also, a lot of people don't get along here. Did you know that a lot of people care about who other people have sex with?" I thought I heard one of the alien's gasp, but I might have been imagining that. "That's speaking about humans, only: what about the Earth itself? Is it fighting us by quaking and exploding? By getting warmer and warmer?

"We're resilient, I'll say that. This planet keeps trying to kill us, but we just keep trying to kill it back, I suppose. I don't think humans can really change. I think that maybe there are some good people, and maybe everyone has the capacity for good, but for every good action there is an equal and negative reaction, and that will be the pattern until the end of time. Perhaps we're all better off just not existing." I paused, then, and leaned on someone's cubicle I had walked to one that was far from mine. I shrugged and said, "Maybe someone else should make the case. I think I'm too much of a cynic to give everyone a chance. I mean, don't get me wrong, there's a lot of good shit on Earth. Like Stanley Kubrick films, and music by Iron & Wine, art by Raoul Duffy, cooking videos, inventions like banana holders (purely for the comedic value)—and even stuff like kayaks and the Muskoka lakes and the Salt Flats and the Taal Volcano. But, I mean, if you exist, then there must be millions of other planets and creatures whose cultures are just as interesting or beautiful or even scary. What can I say? If the Federation deems our planet destructive or destructible, who am I to say that it isn't? I mean, they're supposed to be all-knowing and stuff, right? It's complicated, but if it were up to me, I'd say follow orders because I don't see us getting much better, quite honestly."

I walked from the desk I was at back to mine and pulled a granola bar out of the drawer. It was one of those ones that are half dipped in yogurt, you know? It was strawberry, which is my favorite. As I stood at my desk eating it, everyone was staring at me. Mostly in disbelief, some in solemn admiration but still in disbelief. It was a strange feeling to be so important and eating a granola bar. Do you know what I mean? The fate of the world was in my hands, but instead of looking important or even worth admiring, I was eating a granola bar. I hope those reading this can understand how surreal a feeling this was; and for something to feel surreal in what you think is a dream is incredible.

It felt like ages before anything else happened, but I knew it couldn't have been too long because I was almost done my granola bar and I usually powered through them. Then, the aliens responded.

"We have come to a decision regarding the destruction of your planet."

I could feel a sharp inhalation from everyone in my office, and an involuntary shrug from my own body. I looked around and found the spinning top that I kept on my desk. It was an homage to the film *Inception,* and I used to spin it around hoping that my day job was just a dream and I could fly out one of the floor-to-ceiling windows, far from my cubicle, at any time. Just for fun, I decided to spin my spinning top, and if you've seen the film *Inception,* then you know what it means when the top falters and then stops spinning.

"Jesus fucking Christ," was all I said before they gave their reply.

"We have decided—" the first speaker was cut off by the voice I recognized as the Ruler.

"Listen, Katie. You're clearly going through some sort of phase, and we think you need some time to, you know, be by yourself and what have you. So, um, we'll be back in a few hundred years to reassess Earth's position in the history of the Galaxy. Basically, this is too depressing for us, and we just eradicated a planet where the people were ingesting nuclear waste which was killing them from the inside out. They didn't even understand the irony. So, yeah, just think over your position in life, and we'll come back to you. In a few thousand years." They seemed to be on their way when the Ruler held back to say one last thing.

"You know, Katie, you present some interesting points, though. Perhaps the Federation is fallible, and Earth shouldn't be destroyed. But, on the other hand, humans are creatures of habit, from what we've observed. They destroy and kill and burn to progress; but, as you said, there's so much beauty on this Earth that it may be a pity to destroy it. We've recommended that once humans have reached maturity the Federation should re-evaluate your planet. You are in a certain place in your human development— rebellious, cynical, ambivalent, selfish. At some point, though, we assume that humans will, to put it simply, grow up. Goodbye, Katie Vega, and Earth."

And on that note, they left. They haven't returned since, and I'm not sure they will in my lifetime. The aftermath of their arrival is well known. There is enough written about it on Facebook and Twitter and all those other websites. Directly after they left, though, I remember everyone started cheering in my office. Everyone hugged each other, and a few people hugged me, but it felt like the type of hug that was so involuntary that I could have been anyone. I shrugged it off internally because it seemed as though I really didn't do anything. I said a lot of horrible things about humans, so I guess I should have expected everyone to be wary of me. I also smoked a couple bowls in front of my coworkers, most of whom did not know that I smoked weed, and my overall nonchalance about the end of the world was probably slightly frightening to the squares I worked with.

I'm not positive how to end this account; the Historical Society told me I could do what I wanted. Well, there's not much to say, and my life after That Day isn't really that important. I basically sold my home in the city and most of my stuff in favor of purchasing a home in the country. I make enough money to get by. People even send me money and letters, sometimes, and thank me for what I said—it was inspiring for some people, I guess. They say I helped them realize that life is too short not to do what you love. I get a lot of death threats and whatnot, but that's neither here nor there because anyone even partially famous gets death threats. I'm pretty much off the grid now, which I realize I was always fine with; I never really had anyone or anything keeping me on the grid.

I guess the moral of this story is that everyone has problems; sometimes your problems work in your benefit, and other times, they don't. Something cheesy I could say here is 'once you discover your truth, you need to stick to it'.

But really, we all make our own morals and decisions, and mine seemed to work out for me. Hopefully yours work out for you. I hope you do well on your assignment, and that the planet doesn't get destroyed in your lifetime, or maybe they will come, and you'll have your moment. Does it matter? Shouldn't you live your life to the fullest anyway? As cheesy as that may seem, I guess that's the better moral: live your life as if the aliens are coming to destroy the planet tomorrow. You'll have fewer regrets that way.

Oh, and by the way, my name isn't Katie Vega. It's Haley Santos. I guess it never really mattered, though, anyway—the message, not the messenger and all that.

A Series of Character Origins (That I Could Use Later)

Name: Sam

Age: 37

Interests and Personality: In the opinions of his last three partners, Sam was borderline sociopathic. He was the kind of guy who loved giving beta at the rock-climbing gym unprovoked. He reads a lot of non-fiction about history's great naval battles and is especially interested in procuring a sailboat when his finances inevitably solidify. He has a favorite fingernail and toenail. He is meticulous about his hair. He sometimes goes to the park and watches people, poorly but therapeutically drawing them as hyperbolic versions of themselves. He doesn't like pineapple on his pizza but will order pizza with anchovies just so he doesn't have to share it. His earliest memory is his mother shaving his head as a baby so that she could dress him up as Charlie Brown for Halloween—he was about two years old. Sometimes he feels the sharp pain of the trimmer cutting his scalp when he's in stressful situations.

Day Job: Works as a personal stylist at a prominent menswear company, but only does this to support himself. His greatest dream is to open up a brewery that specializes in acai berry-based alcohol, from liquor infusions to flavored beer. He believes there's a huge market for acai berry-flavored things.

He has been denied by the bank for this loan six times.

Openly: Wants to make a case directly to all the bankers at a branch under threat of death if no one agrees to help him. Is willing to torture psychologically in order to achieve his goal.

Secretly: Has reached a breaking point. Feels as though he'll never get a real chance to prove himself, and so rationalizes that he needs to create his chance. Wants to prove that he's worthy of success and happiness.

Do they like to get their hands dirty? No.

Backstory/First Take:
Sam walked into the bank, thinking: "Today is the day. Lucky 7."

Patting the gun in his belt and tapping his portfolio against his leg, Sam walked through the metal detector. The alarm went off, but Sam, having been to this bank often, knew the security guard on duty was awful at his job. Sam took off his belt and held it up for the guard to see.

"Yeah, yeah, no worries. Go ahead," the guard muttered, waving his hand dismissively and returning to the newspaper. Sam noticed he was reading the comics section.

"Oh! I used to *love* Marmaduke," he announced. The security guard looked up at him with a face that said, "Why are you still here". Sam smiled politely and wished him a good day, making his way into the main offices of the bank.

The bank itself was housed in a converted old building, years passing making its original purpose miscellaneous. It smelled like stale bread and coffee and employed a similar color scheme. The terrazzo tile Sam walked on shied away from his light footsteps after years of berating from hard heels and deep exfoliation. Sam tried not to look at his feet but instead ahead of him, confidently, unsuccessfully.

Do they know they're the villain? Yes.

Name: Marc

Age: 30

Interests and Personality (outside of Villainy):
Woodworking, reading various religious and anti-religious
texts, psychology papers, having bonfires on his large
country property. Marc is an artist in his spare time and
likes to hang out with his friends. He is relatively awkward
around women. He has had a few girlfriends before and isn't
a virgin, but he isn't very good at talking to women, and
hasn't been the instigator of most of his sexual experiences.
All these experiences ended poorly, making Marc mistrustful
of women in general. Ultimately, he is a country boy, and
enjoys being in the wilderness, and participating in nature.
He is self-sufficient on his property. He has many friends,
friends who would not expect him to behave the way he did.

Day Job: He was gifted the property he lives on when his
mother died several years ago. His friend, Michael, runs a
construction company in town, and sometimes Marc helps
out. He likes helping out his friends and is the person they call
if they need some work done around their properties that they
can't do, and often he gets paid in food. Marc makes a lot of art
in his spare time, which he sells. His art is popular amongst
artists because of his unconventional media. He uses things he
finds around his property to create interesting pieces.

Openly: He's just trying to look out for himself and make
sure she isn't like all the others.

Secretly: He wants revenge on all the women who broke
him with their unfaithfulness and abandonment.

Do they like to get their hands dirty? Yes

Backstory: "I said, 'I don't know why you're so quiet'. Are you sleeping again?" He lifted her chin and noticed that her neck was limp. He calmly put his finger under her nose and, noticing she was still breathing, decided to let her sleep a little longer. She looked so peaceful; he didn't want to wake her. He walked away from her and towards the small table in the boathouse, where they were currently housed. He let his fingers linger on the small items that littered the table; a comb with her hairs woven between the tines, his glass of water, a small notebook full of writing only he could read. He stopped at the end of the table and, after drumming his fingers in an indiscernible pattern for several seconds, spoke again to Catherine.

"I don't know why, but whenever I think of us, I think of this story my mom used to read me. It's about true love and intestinal fortitude in the face of fear." He didn't know if she could hear him but resigned himself to the fact that her subconscious mind would pick up his words. He meandered through their shared space, smiling sadly at the beautiful paintings they had made together, now tinged with negativity. He settled in his usual chair, opposite Catherine.

"It's amazing what you can find on the internet nowadays. The story is recorded on this random blog I found. I didn't even have to look for very long," he scrolled through his phone until he found the aforementioned blog.

"Sometimes I get a little afraid that you won't pass these tests, Catherine," he looked off into the distance dramatically, performing more for himself than any real audience. "Sometimes I worry about you, about your subconscious and its hold on you. I know you can overcome all of this adversity, though." He looked at her, still asleep. Resting. "You're so entrenched in these pre-conceived notions of life—just like the first girls in this story. Maybe your subconscious will do something good for you and internalize the true love in this story."

Do they know they're the villain? No.

The Time My Dad Met Douglas Coupland

An essay by James Michael Turner

Let me preface this story by telling you a bit about Douglas Coupland. He is a rather famous Canadian author whose titles number in the dozens. One of my favorite books of his, *jPod*, was actually made into a television series, though it did not garner much critical acclaim; in my opinion, the show did not do the book justice, but that's neither here nor there. His books are known to be profound and heart wrenching while being darkly funny, making them poignant representations of real life with a degree of the phenomenal the reader never questions. He also paints and sculpts, with many different pieces on display, including one memorial to the War of 1812 in downtown Toronto. Despite his seeming profundity, one does not always believe the author him or herself is as deep as their body of work implies.

My father would normally make up some context for why the two met where they did, saying he was simply visiting an old teenage hang-out, or attempting to be one with nature.

But as I got older, I knew the real reason he was sitting at the edge of a cliff in British Columbia on a windy day over tumultuous water. My father was going to commit suicide. My mother was the one who told me the truth and insisted that my father was a different person then; he had been hopeless and depressed, with no career prospects and a wife who was too good for him. People without a clinical diagnosis might take these setbacks and use them as inspiration, launching themselves into a new life filled with job applications, night classes, and other things that society tells you you should do when you feel sad. My father struggled with depression, though and since it was mostly untreated, he preferred to self-medicate. This was simply how he dealt with his feelings before he met Douglas Coupland, and to quote *Jesus Christ Superstar*, "If your slate is clean then you can throw stones".

The day my father was to make his suicide attempt the weather reports called for high waves and thunderstorms. His plan, he told my mother, who later told me, had been to dive from the 200-meter cliff onto the rocks below and hopefully bash his head open; if he did not land the right way for his skull to crack open, he would surely drown in the unsteady waters. He went to Alcoholics Anonymous meetings before he met my mother, and some of the people he had met at the meetings had tried to kill themselves, but their methods seemed like madness; either too painful or too likely to fail. When my father was a teenager, he would cliff dive with his friends, so he may have rationalized this spectacular scheme by believing the final dive would remind him of his youth, letting him die on a joyful, nostalgic note. But there was something beneath this reasoning that made it clear there was more to this choice, and when my mother would ask, he would only say he "thought it was the easiest and least painful of all the methods [he] could think of".

He drove north out of Vancouver, where he and my mother were living, in the old '57 Chevy his father had given him and parked in a small clearing where people once seemed to park but had not for a while. He walked from his car to the cliff and sat with his feet dangling off the edge, staring out at the ocean with a completely blank mind. In a heartbeat, though, he would always say, his mind became as tumultuous as the water below, pushing and pulling him in one direction that screamed 'jump', and the other direction that screamed 'don't'. When telling me this story he did not include the part about pushing and pulling, just that his mind was blank. As I said before, I did not know my father had intended to commit suicide at some point in this story until I was older, but my mother, when I was old enough, was my resource for these details. I may have asked my father about it once or twice, and though it had been at least fifteen years since it happened, he still seemed embarrassed about it, though I assured him I was not judging him; I understood that it would have been difficult for him to really open up to me, which was why I would go to my mother for information. As I write this, though, I have found a much better source for context on my father. Still, the dialogue between Douglas and my father is somewhat lost in time; only the two of them know exactly what was said, and even they are not infallible.

My father sat there for what seemed like hours, and it was during one of these moment-hours that Douglas Coupland, like a woodland nymph, stepped out of the forest behind my father. My dad would joke that he had hoped the noise signaled a thing of beauty, like a bobcat or a deer, but it was instead Douglas Coupland in a multi-colored, pastel rain poncho and hiking gear. The rain was not there yet, but it was coming, and my dad said he could feel it in the air like you could feel heat a foot from a bonfire. Some people may be eloquent upon seeing someone somewhat famous, but my father was not articulate under pressure, and the words that came out of his mouth were something like: "What the fuck are you doing here, Douglas Coupland?" to which Douglas

Coupland, an astute surveyor of human emotion and action who *was* articulate under pressure, replied, "Well, not what the fuck *you're* doing here," and walked up to my father.

"You know who I am, apparently, but I don't know you and I insist on knowing before you die," the author stated, putting his hand out to my now-standing father. "Anyone with a '57 Bel-Air in that condition deserves respect." My father shook Douglas' hand and introduced himself as Mike Turner after considering lying about his name. My father would say that anyone who could name a Chevy by the year, even if they were just guessing, deserved respect and that he felt Douglas would know if Mike Turner was not his real name.

Douglas maintains that he motioned to the edge of the cliff using the universally understood hand gestures, but my father would disagree in his version of the story. As a result of the misunderstanding, my father would describe himself as being wary and, in an attempt to diffuse the tension, the ever-tactful Douglas Coupland declared, "You were *just* sitting there, what makes now so different? You think I'm going to push you or something?" My father was taken aback by how brash the author was, but then shrugged it off and sat down. Though the two had just met, he would say authoritatively, he knew he could trust Douglas and was sure that Douglas felt the same way.

"How do I know what you're doing on this cliff on probably the most dangerous day to *be* sitting on this cliff?" Douglas asked this in such a way that it seemed to my father he was hypothesizing the way a scientist might. "Well, it kind of radiates from someone like you, but that's probably not exactly true. I guess I saw it in you because I've seen it before, and I know what to look for. Also, what else would someone be doing on a day like this, and here?" He said this with a sort of sarcasm he let bleed into his next statement. "So, why do you think you should die? Keep in mind, I may use this for a novel later so be completely honest; 'Life is infinitely stranger than anything the mind could invent' and all that."

Anyone who has ever wanted to do something knows speaking about that action is powerful and can deter or encourage one to pursue said action. My father was being asked to reflect upon his decision, which is often the first step in the process of deterrence. In the child-friendly version of the story, my father would omit this part, but since I know it now, I will include it because it adds another layer.

The words poured out of my father in quick succession. "My wife is too good for me. I have a dead-end job. I feel like I lost my talent for selling years ago. I blame myself for my father's death. I can't—" Douglas interrupted my father, who was flailing.

"Okay, okay. Let's go through everything, one at a time, and see if we can't work this out. I know you probably have a lot to say so we should probably start discussing." This was the third time my father was surprised by Douglas, and certainly not the last. They began to talk and talked away the better part of the afternoon. It wasn't completely one-sided; Douglas asked questions and told his own stories, like any good artist. Douglas gave my father a sense of security that only comes when people share their life experiences—there's something about conversing with a stranger that allows a person to open up, which I've always found oddly comforting. My father felt as though his struggle was not one that had to be faced alone for the first time in his life, and this was invaluable.

After talking about their lives and problems, the two began to talk about life and its problems. This is where my father would jump to after the two met. My father would tell me something different every time. Once the conversation was about how cooking was a metaphor for life, another conversation was about books that the two liked that weren't Douglas Coupland's. But my favorite conversation, at least as I grew older and heard the adult version of the story, was their conversation about God, and that's the one I will recount here.

"Well, Mike, we're around the same age, and so I want to ask you something: Do you believe in God?" Douglas looked at my father intensely, making him feel like he couldn't lie. My father replied that he did not and followed a wave with his eyes from the horizon to the rocks below. In his periphery, he saw Douglas nodding.

"What about you?" My father asked, trying not to seem rude. Douglas clearly had an opinion and my father was interested in what he had to say.

"It's curious. I feel as though our generation is the first generation to truly live without God and yet the generation that needs God the most. We have no great war—at least, not one worth fighting. How can we be expected to believe in God when God seems like a convention of the simple minded? Maybe, though," Douglas posited, picking up little rocks from the ground and launching them into the sea, "you wouldn't be trying to kill yourself if you believed in God. Suicide is a deadly sin in Christianity, of course, but also because you might be more secure with yourself and have a larger community to rely on, not just strangers in forests. Have you tried therapy?" He stopped launching rocks when he ran out of rocks in his general vicinity.

My father took in what he was saying but decided to answer the question before proceeding with the conversation. "I tried therapy, but I just couldn't get into it. I don't know exactly what it was, but I suppose I just couldn't open up. It was also after a... spectacular, if I can use that word, incident after which I had to do therapy, so... I guess I wasn't really into it from the beginning. No one wants to do things people make them do, right?" My father said this as he watched the ripples in the water dissipate around the spots where Douglas' rocks had landed.

"You probably had a bad shrink; they aren't all aces. I had a friend whose therapist she would refer to by his first name because he was more of a friend than a therapist—he made her feel as though she shouldn't be ashamed to go to therapy." It was at this point that my father watched Douglas Coupland dig into his jacket pocket and pull out a joint and a match, which he lit against a rock. "Puff, puff, pass, man," Douglas warned, exhaling. Needless to say, I only learned about the marijuana smoking later. Douglas handed the marijuana to my father, who hadn't smoked for several years. He inhaled poorly which resulted in a coughing fit. Douglas smiled.

"We would all be better off with God, or with some sort of belief in God, and yet there is extreme difficulty and pain, I would say, in such a belief. Imagine what God's existence would signify; namely a loss of control, even if destiny and God are not mutually inclusive," my father passed back the joint and as Douglas inhaled, he chimed in.

"Which is odd, considering we as a generation tend to outsource our production."

Douglas nodded and held onto the joint for a minute, letting it burn in his hand. "God makes it impossible to really make any mistakes. I knew a guy—actually, the girl who had a great therapist's boyfriend—who adamantly objected to Christian teaching because it allowed for anyone to enter heaven if they were repentant, and some people, he would say, probably didn't deserve forgiveness. Child rapists, war lords, et al. But to really answer your question, I don't necessarily believe in God, but there is a certain philosophy that I appreciate and, in some ways, adhere to."

Whenever I think of my life and God's place in it, I think of this same philosophy. It is a wager proposed by Blaise Pascal, a prominent mathematician from the 17th century. I did research on this wager after my father told me about it and I was old enough to use a computer, which prepared me for the philosophy course I took this year. The wager is divided into four parts, and can be found anywhere on the internet, but I will include it here for some measure of continuity and to simplify it in a way:

Option 1: God exists; you live as if God exists.
> You win the ultimate prize: that is, going to heaven.

Option 2: God exists; you live as if God does not exist.
> You lose: you go to Hell, or whatever you believe the negative afterlife is.

Option 3: God does not exist; you live as if God exists. No harm, no foul.
> You, presumably, lived your life as a good person, so you benefit from that.

Option 4: God does not exist; you live as if God does not exist.
> Again, no harm, no foul, because there is no negative to your afterlife.

This wager is interesting because it yields no right answers. What I feel is the ideal is to live as though God does exist, that is, be a good person, and perhaps you will benefit later. If you do not benefit in the end, then you probably encountered some sort of good karma that benefitted you in your life; but then again, perhaps not. Either way, bad choices can be made up for often, by which I mean that I believe karma *does* exist. My father believed that good yields good, and he passed his belief onto me; we are usually very critical of our parents' beliefs, no matter how much we love them, and I continue to examine this belief and find little to no fault in it. Cause and effect, as it were.

After the joint was finished and disposed of, the two zoned out and watched the waves. After a while, Douglas turned to my father and said this:

"I have a plan, Mike. I'm going to refer you to my therapist, who just happens to be covered by our province's wonderful healthcare system." My father always quoted him in a way that can only be described as 'snarky'. "I really think you should go see him. He's great, Bruce. Quite a nice guy. But there is another thing I think would be quite an interesting undertaking for the two of us." My father heard what Douglas said, but could only think 'Jesus Christ, when was the last time I smoked this much? I should lie the fuck down'.

But instead of speaking this aloud he simply said, "What?" and then Douglas began to suggest something my father was not expecting.

"I'm going to call you every week, same Bat time, same Bat channel, whatever we decide is the best, and you're going to tell me everything. I feel very invested in your future, Mike, and I want to make sure you don't kill yourself. You can tell me anything—what you did that day, or that same day ten years ago; where you were when Elvis died, what your childhood was like. I want to know everything. I want your life story. I know it sounds sort of 'sell me your soul'-ish, but really, I kind of have a bit of writer's block, you know? It's always good to have extra inspiration. Also, it will probably be therapeutic for you. Probably."

Never the one to miss an opportunity, Douglas probably saw this as a chance to write a real-life story and somewhat embellish it while maintaining the, well, reality of it. My father, after thinking about it for a minute, agreed, unable to say no. Though at face-value it appeared Douglas only wanted to make money off my father's life story, my father sensed that there as more to this than it seemed. The two continued to talk until about three am, when they parted ways and the marijuana had pretty much worn off. They decided that

Douglas would call my father at six pm every Tuesday, and the two exchanged numbers. Although my father did not think Douglas would call him every week, he knew he was better for believing someone cared enough to do so.

My earliest memory of Douglas, then, is from my sixth birthday. I know I had met him at least a dozen times before, but that's my earliest memory of him. He told me I could call him Doug or Dougie, whatever my mouth could formulate, until I was twelve, and after that it would have to be Douglas. But my six-year-old mouth couldn't properly articulate Doug or Dougie, so for about six years I called him 'Doggie' or 'Dog', but he didn't seem to mind until I turned twelve and tried to call him Doggie as a joke. He and my father talked every Tuesday for about twenty years, but there was never, explicitly, a book. My mother feels as though the book *All Families are Psychotic* is loosely based on my father's life—very loosely. If you have read the book, maybe you understand why my father was depressed and why he drank. After I was born, three years into their talks, my father beat back his depression enough to finish the college degree that he had started, making him a Certified Public Accountant. There are pictures of his graduation on the walls of my home, with me as a little baby in my mother's arms. I think I was proud of him, even then. My father always had a penchant for math, and though Douglas offered to refer him to some of his friends, my father refused, preferring not to get mixed up in the seedy underbelly of West Coast writers; Douglas maintained that writers usually got paid under the table anyway.

My father's story is a pretty sensational one. I remember, after hearing the story when I was about ten or twelve, the PG version of the story that is, I didn't really believe it—I thought maybe they were just close friends from high school or something. But then I noticed my father going into his study every Tuesday at the same time and staying in there for at least an hour. My father is someone I admire for all he has accomplished and overcome, and it is difficult to imagine him as the depressed and heartbroken man he was before I was born. I suppose part of that is thanks to Douglas, but most of it has to do with my father, who is, in a word, my hero.

Maybe Douglas came into my father's life at the right time, the perfect moment between death and life when my father realized he could either fish or cut bait, as some people say. I used to think that Douglas saved my father's life, but I'm not so sure anymore. Maybe he just reminded my father that there is more than one reason to live, and more than one reason to die, but dwelling on the reasons only wastes time. Douglas always told me to end an essay with a good quote, but my parents agreed that was played out. Here's a quote, anyway, said by famous thespian Orson Welles: "If you want a happy ending, that depends, of course, on where you stop your story."

Dear Ms. Volchuck,

I first want to apologize for not being in class. I sincerely enjoy Writer's Craft and it is one of the classes I've missed the most in my time away from school. I am sure that Mrs. Callum has explained my situation to you, but I just briefly wanted to explain exactly why I haven't been in class and was unable to write the intended final paper by its initial due date.

As you may have discerned from reading this essay, my father drank for more than half of his life, and last August he contracted liver cancer. It wasn't just the drinking, but it didn't help, of course. Although chemotherapy was helping for a while, two months ago it stopped making a difference, and my father took a turn for the worse. The week he died he was in a coma, but the week before that, with the seemingly large amount of clarity only the dying have, he told us that we should take away his life support if he was comatose for any longer than four days. We fought him on it, but in vain, because he was a stubborn man and refused to change his mind, offering to make anyone who would fulfil his wish his power of attorney instead of my mother. The day we took him off life support was the worst day of my life so far, and I am currently in therapy trying to cope with his death.

Mrs. Callum told me that when she asked you what I should write about, you said to write about the most pivotal moment in my life. Writing about my father's death would not only have been too difficult now, but I also do not know what kind of effect it will have on me. But this story about my father meeting Douglas Coupland—maybe you can understand why I consider that story more important to my personal narrative than something that happened in my own life time. Without this story, I probably wouldn't be who I am today, and my father wouldn't have been who he was. Death is usually the turning point in a story, as I've learned in your class, but this wasn't necessarily my denouement.

My father taught me that anything can be overcome, whether it is a difficult piece in band or depression, and whether it is completely or just enough. I appreciate everything he taught me. He was an amazing father and did the best he could. We didn't see eye to eye every moment we had together, and it is only now I realize that I should have listened more and talked less, but it doesn't matter. Before he died, we got to have a talk about our past and my future. I loved my father, and I miss him and everything he was and wasn't.

The best metaphor I can find for life is that it is like a cigarette. It burns slowly when you're letting it sit, but when you're enjoying it, it burns so quickly. I don't smoke, of course, I'm only seventeen, but I think the point is clear. Time flies.

Thank you, again, for the opportunity to make up the final project. I hope you enjoyed this essay, Ms. Volchuck.

Sincerely,
James Michael Turner

P.S. Douglas recorded everything my father told him during their phone calls and compiled the stories into a book for me. Memories are fallible, of course, but recorders help. Most of this story was included in the anthology and was my only source. I know I'm supposed to source my work, but I didn't know if the anthology was an interview or just a book— it was all very informal. I hope this is enough.

The Devil You Know

–By S.T.

"In retrospect I probably should've bailed on the whole party and stayed home and watched, I don't know, *Clerks* or something," Sean Miller told me a year after his incredible encounter with the devil incarnate, in this lifetime going by the name Morningstar. "But I did learn from the whole experience and I don't really regret it, as fucked up as that sounds." The young man pulls out a cigarette and lights it, inhaling deeply. We are sitting in the countryside, on his deck, attached to a house he bought with the money he earned from the Devil.

The first thing I noted about Sean Miller were his looks. He is classically handsome, dark skin and dark hair with light eyes providing a contrast that would draw anyone in. Not only blessed with charming features and an athletic physique, Sean is also inquisitive, empathetic, and a self-proclaimed introvert—the sum-total of many people's ideal traits. Sean was accepted to MIT on a full scholarship for his innovations in the field of lyophilization technology and was off on summer break when he met Morningstar. His fatal flaw, though, as even he will tell you, is that he is apathetic almost to the point of disorder.

"I think that's why she picked me. She knew I had the stomach to do her dirty work for money. Most people would quit doing what I did after their first client." Sean Miller, as most people know, was coerced by the Devil into running errands. It usually involved delivering packages for people who had sold their souls to the devil for various things.

"I once delivered a puppy to someone. I found out later that the same puppy would go on to win some award that means a lot to dog owners. I mean, I could be judgmental about it, but I could also just admit that to each his own."

Sean has always been forthcoming with journalists about his experience. When I *politely* asked him to share a story that I hadn't heard before, he scoffed and said, "Well, one time, I got to visit a celebrity, I won't disclose who, but I was treated pretty well. He and I smoked some 'devil's lettuce', and I gave him his package. He let me stay while he opened it. This is maybe my favourite story to tell because it's the only one I got something valuable from. When he opened the box, there was nothing in it, but he nodded solemnly and thanked me. Not many people really thanked me." Sean leaned forward in his chair and looked out into the distance and explained, "When I asked him why he was thanking me and asked if I could pry about what he had been given, he smirked and told me that what he had been given was the knowledge about what happens after we die. We ended up having a conversation which led to me writing my book of essays."

The book of essays in question was on *the New York Times* Bestseller list for four months straight. I read the book, and it *is* powerful. The question of what happens after we die is only one of the topics broached in the anthology. He also talks about creativity, and family, and a slew of other themes, making it highly recommended by myself and several members of the team here at Killing It Publications. Sean doesn't mention this anecdote about the celebrity in his book, and during our interview I wondered what the answer was.

"He never told me, actually. I understand why—I really shouldn't have even asked. We'll all know soon enough, right?" He looked at me and smiled widely.

"Possibly the most interesting thing about your whole experience," I began before pouring myself a glass of wine, which had been offered earlier, "is how you remain positive in post. I mean, you hurt a lot of people—people who came after you in court, in the media, in person. How do you keep going after something like that?" The answer, I'll admit, caught me by surprise.

"You know, what always bothered me about people going after me was that I didn't do anything wrong. I was doing what I was getting paid to do. I harbored no ill will towards any of the people I delivered to, even after they took me to court or tried to attack me.

"I took the job under false pretenses—I thought I was going to be a simple courier, toting packages from one place to another and getting paid for it. I needed a summer job to pay for certain expenses I had accrued. I stopped doing drugs out of boredom because I was busy all the time and I got to meet a lot of interesting people, not including the people who wanted to hurt me. Those people are the kinds of people that didn't know what they were asking for or what they were giving up.

"If you ask your parents for a dog, and in your head, you're hoping for a golden retriever but in the end you get a pug, the reality is that you were giving in to expectation, which is actually the most harmful thing a person can do. My friend Mark, he used to do a lot of shows as a musician, and he would invite people, myself included, to shows and sometimes we wouldn't show up. Alan, our buddy, used to feel really bad when he couldn't make a show, but Mark straight up told him that he had zero expectations when he invited people out and that Alan shouldn't feel bad at all because Mark was confident enough in his performing to do what he loved without his friends being there.

"So, I'll say to you the same thing I said in court. If those people expected different answers than the ones they got, it was because they were too wrapped up in their fantasies of what they would get to appreciate what they were asking for. Selling your soul to the Devil for a fucking promotion, to me, sounds wretched, but that was most often what I was delivering to people. The people who didn't like it were the ones who realized that they wasted their souls on something as stupid as work, and the people who were okay with it felt they had nothing to lose anyway and ended up using their promotions for good. I mean, you can only really look at this stuff on a case by case basis, but I think you understand what I'm saying, Sam."

I did. I completely understood.

"The long and the short of it is, I relinquished expectation and began to care only about what was actually occurring in reality. In reality, those people were lashing out at me because they were unhappy. I wasn't unhappy at all—I made a fuckton of money, met some fascinating people, and did a lot of super fun shit all while maintaining a good enough GPA to keep my scholarship and graduate with honors. Ultimately, working for Morningstar was a really good time for me once I realized that expecting only good things to happen and relishing in the good things that happen were two different things."

I didn't know what to expect when I shook hands with the man who serviced the Devil, but I came to learn a lot from Sean Miller in the short time we spent together. He welcomed me into his home and allowed me insight into his complex experience with possibly the most complex figure in human history. I asked him many questions, the lot of them being findable wherever you listen to KIP podcasts, but the most important question, the question on everyone's minds, I never got an answer to.

"So, how do we know that you didn't sell your soul for your seminal novel, and incredible successes in general?"

"You don't, but it doesn't really matter anyway, does it?"

Experiment 518

"Experiment five-one-eight seems to be behaving normally, sir. The subject goes through the routine Dr. Winters and I created for it and does not object to any of the tasks we request it to perform. All in all, I believe that the subject will be able to be released into the world soon. This day in age, people are not averse to the idea of androids roaming around and getting jobs, et cetera... At least that's what our anthropologists and sociologists tell us."

Dr. Flounder and Dr. Winters had been working a very long time on this android, whom they affectionately named Biff. When they were first signed on for the project, they had not been enthusiastic; they had found there wasn't a ton of money in androids at the time due to a lot of different ethical boundaries. The two of them had worked together to practically write the book on androids. They had written papers on Artificial Brain Formation, Hypothetical Extremity Generation, and, their most popular, The Effects of Berries on Non-Water-Based Life Forms. The team of Winters and Flounder had been responsible for the genesis of the Android Equality Alliance (AEA) and the Researchers and Scientists Researching Science Union (RSRSU). They were so important to the scientific community that when immortality was finally achieved, they were the first ones to receive the serum by the RSRSU, free of charge. Naturally Verner and Sons had no choice but to hire the two and lock them into a 70-year contract before any of the other Golden 500 Companies could.

Werner Verner Senior knew androids were the way of the future, and his last act as CEO of Verner and Sons was to hire doctors Winters and Flounder to begin work on a functioning Android. Werner Verner Junior, most often referred to as Junior, carried on his father's wish and, though he didn't agree with the creation of androids, allowed Winters and Flounder from eight to ten percent of the yearly budget, just as his father had. Junior had been in his mid-40s when his father died, and was now pushing 70, with a full head of grey hair to prove his age. Calling him 'Junior' would've been a cruel joke if it hadn't been so important to him; it was so important to him that he didn't even keep the tradition up for his own children, giving them unique names so he could continue to be the only Junior around. He would visit the lab twice a week to see how much progress the two had made in their experiments. This week, he had been by every day to follow the new developments; primarily, a working Android.

"So, what you're saying is that we have created a real working person? Does it think for itself and all that?" Junior was skeptical, having grown up a member of the Neo-Catholic faith, but he believed that the sciences were God's way of raising humans back to the way they were before Adam and Eve 'ruined it for all of us' (a popular conspiracy theory nowadays). He was interested in Biff for reasons outside of faith or, really, outside of ethics.

"Yes, sir. Biff—er, Experiment five-one-eight, that is, can do anything you or I can do. We're even working on making him skin, so he can blend in with humans by showering, swimming, basically interacting with water in a safer way. As of right now, he is a little alarming to look at if you're not used to him..."

Junior was watching the android in his glass cell. He quickly corrected himself by referring to the enclosed space Experiment 518 was situated in as a *room*. The word 'cell' implied imprisonment, and Junior had never considered that the situation *could* be imprisonment. Biff got everything he wanted or needed—how could he even conceptualize a lack of freedom if this life was all he knew? Junior turned to Dr. Flounder and asked, "Could I have a conversation with him?" I would like to see the true extent of the android's capabilities."

Junior was not so different from his father; both were opinionated and, to put it simply, demanding, making the mildness of his query surprising. Flounder said, "By all means, sir," and Junior went into the room where the android was being held—living—and began to talk to him.

Biff had a television in his room and was very into musicals when Junior first met him. He was watching *Chitty Chitty Bang Bang* when Junior, Doctors Winters and Flounder, and several security guards who insisted on protecting the CEO and owner of Verner and Sons, one of the most successful companies of Earth and the Adjacent Planets, entered the room. Biff hardly noticed them—he was so entranced by the film. He had seen this film at least ten times in the last week and was looking forward to his favorite scene, even though it was towards the end of the film.

"Excuse me, Experime—Biff? I believe that's what you're known as around here." Junior had been given a chair by one of the security guards and was sitting behind Biff. The Android was sitting opposite the television, quite close to the screen, but uncaring, because he found out earlier that week that every part of him was indestructible. He was quite sad to discover most of the people in the musicals he watched were long dead, having lived almost 150 years before he gained consciousness. He turned his chair around and faced Junior, knowing the conversation they would have would require Biff follow formal social rules, the knowledge of which had been installed by Winters and Flounder.

"Yes, sir. They call me Biff. I'm to understand it's because of Dr. Flounder's love of the *Back to the Future* film franchises of the 1980s."

Junior laughed, "Is that why? Wonderful. But I came to talk to you, and learn about you, Biff. They tell me you're going through a phase right now that involves you watching and re-watching 20th and 21st century musicals. What brought this on?"

Biff looked around his room. He had pictures of people who had come through his room and his life, pictures of plants and animals, he had a dresser with nothing in it, a book case with a few classic fictions on it, a bed that he didn't need because he didn't need to sleep, and a television with many different film files. He simply had to navigate through the TV's menu screens, which he could do from his mind, to play a film. He enjoyed his life in his room but felt very sheltered. After what he expected were a few moments, he answered Junior's question simply.

"Nothing in particular, sir. The television program I was watching one day had a reference from a 20th century musical, and I felt as though I should watch that musical to understand the reference. Then, I found more musicals and became more interested in watching them." Biff felt joy remembering the first time he had watched *Singing in the Rain*, and if Verner Werner Junior hadn't spoken, Biff would've stayed in that memory instead of falling back to Earth and his room.

"Wonderful, wonderful," said Verner Werner Junior. He never expected the Android to speak so much like a human. He sounded familiar, as well—Junior later found out that, as a joke, the two doctors—after a night of drinking and watching *The Matrix*, a movie the two doctors believed was one of the best of all time—had formulated Biff's voice out of the voice and speech patterns of Keanu Reeves.

There was a knock on the glass wall of Biff's room from Dr. Flounder. He mouthed the words "Can we come in?" to Junior, who waved them in. Biff struggled to keep his face from reacting to the impending interaction.

"We just wanted to show you a few of the things that Biff can do besides converse realistically."

Junior leaned back in his chair and shrugged. "By all means," he mumbled.

"Biff, who is this man you're speaking to?"

Biff opened his mouth wide, and seemingly out of a speaker in the back of his throat he said, "This is Werner Verner the fourth, son of Werner Verner the third. He is the CEO and Chairman of Verner and Sons, a Golden 500 company specializing in pharmaceuticals and clean energy." Biff closed his mouth.

Dr. Winters walked to Biff and sternly whispered to speak properly and not be lazy. He turned and smiled at Junior.

"Biff, what do you know about Junior specifically?"

Biff paused for a moment, tinkering with his own programming to make sure his face stopped emoting. He learned he could do this after the two doctors began using negative reinforcement to correct his manners and the 'attitude' his facial expressions betrayed.

"Verner Werner Junior is a member of the Neo-Catholic faith. He is a licensed priest of this faith and preaches at his local church on a rotational basis with Trisha Howard, Ying Gutenberg, Kyle Ho-Barrister, and Marcia Holland. Verner Werner Junior has written a book, *Miracles in Everyday Life* and been featured as an author for several others, such as *Neo-Catholicism and You: Conversion Stories to Inspire*, and *The Businessperson's Guide to Religion and Business*.

He has a passion for gardening and the outdoors, which is why he was responsible for Verner and Sons' pivot to clean energy when he took over, as he said in an article for *Wired Magazine*, written by H. W. Cellar for the March issue seven years ago. He has four children and has been married for 50 years to Alex Kong. They live—"

"That's enough Biff."

"Mostly in New York city, but they winter in Florida—"

"That's enough Biff!" Flounder motioned in the air, interacting with a screen that his contact lenses produced (state of the art, of course). Biff stopped speaking abruptly when his mouth snapped shut. In addition to manually stopping Biff's speech, Flounder also added his customary pain-sensor flare to punish Biff for, presumably, embarrassing him in front of Junior. Biff had done this on purpose, of course, and had counted on the abuse, but didn't care. He enjoyed making them look bad.

"We can assure you, sir, that these malfunctions are few and far between," Winters piped up, shooting a glare at Biff.

"No worries, I understand," Junior said. "Now, can I interact with the android on my own? I know my own history; I don't really need to hear it talk more about me."

Biff smiled internally and the doctors sputtered out of the room, saying things like, "Of course sir" and "You're the boss".

Junior looked at Biff and smiled warmly. "I think we were talking about musicals before we were interrupted. Do you like anything else? What else do you do here all day?"

Biff reinstated his facial emotive functions but remained a bit guarded. "Well, I've been listening to a lot of 21st century rap music. In the 21st century, rappers seemed to have something to say." Biff tried to smile but stopped when he remembered that to some his smile was sort of unnerving.

"Oh, yes! 21st century rap was my favorite when I was growing up. Kendrick and J. Cole... Even Bow Wow's comeback album in the mid-20s was really good. Pop music in general from that era was better than our pop music now. All this experimental djent-rap coming out makes my head hurt." The two watched each other closely. Biff could tell that Junior was excited, remembering all the music he had loved in his younger years and loved still—music that his children and grandchildren didn't seem to care about.

Biff decided to loosen up a little and used his mind to start playing music in the room. The room flooded with Logic's voice, and both Biff and Junior nodded their heads to the beat.

"I really liked his first album, especially with the Tarantino dialogues and stuff!" Junior yelled over the music.

"I found it worked really well, too! And it showed the fun side of Logic that we didn't necessarily see in his albums afterwards!" Biff paused for a second to enjoy an upcoming line. "I like that he talks about 21st century America. I know he was from Baltimore. Isn't that where you're from, sir?"

"Very good! Yes, that's where I grew up, but I was born in Rockville."

"Your mother was visiting family when she went into labor with you, right? That's why you were born in Rockville and not Baltimore." Biff turned down the music but was set on letting the song finish.

"How do you know that?" Junior seemed a little suspicious. Biff knew he had to quell any feelings of discomfort if he was going to continue the conversation. "You mentioned it in an interview once. And so did your mother. In one of the rare interviews she did, of course." Biff watched Junior nod and smile, in Biff's opinion, sadly.

"She didn't do a lot of interviews, no. But she was really a vibrant woman. She liked to party, too. She was very New York City. Alex says she reminded him of Carrie from *Sex in the City*." Junior laughed. "She had the closet to match, too."

"HBO is responsible for a lot of good television. I haven't watched much besides *Westworld*—the doctors insisted—and *The Sopranos*, but I plan on getting to *Sex and the City* and *Game of Thrones* eventually."

Biff watched Junior's face light up at what he assumed to be the opportunity to speak about things he was passionate about. Biff imagined that there weren't a lot of people Junior could speak candidly and comfortably to about things that he liked. Biff could relate; the doctors only talked to him about things they could quantify for their research.

Junior and Biff spoke about Junior's childhood for a while, eventually coming back to music and branching off into conversations about musicians-turned-actors and the importance of a hype-person. Their conversation ended when Junior's keeper came to the lab to remind him he had to eat dinner with the 'board'. Junior seemed reluctant to leave, and Biff was reluctant to let him go. Junior promised he'd be back, and Biff started to plan a scenario where Biff would leave his facial emote sensors on when the doctors hurt him. Not knowing what to do, Biff said that he would be glad to have Junior back and offered him his hand.

"A handshake? I think we're past that!" Junior joked. He hugged the android goodbye and Biff smiled a big, toothy, unnerving grin. Junior left with the rest of the people present, leaving Biff alone to continue watching his films.

After a few minutes alone, the thoughts crept in. Biff battled back the thoughts that said his plan would never work, that this would always be his life, and that there was nothing more to have. That Junior was a business man, that it didn't matter that an android was experiencing pain at the hands of his prized doctors. Fortunately for Biff, no matter what terrible things he could imagine, for the first time in his short life he had hope. The last few hours with Junior would be logged in Biff's perfect memory alongside his other good memories, hidden in a secret place in his brain that the Doctors couldn't access during their evaluations, and couldn't delete later.

Biff turned back to the television to see his favorite and least favorite scene of the film. He watched with dismay and elation as Truly behaved like a robot and sang to the Baron and Baroness of Vulgaria. He watched and re-watched the scene as he did every time he watched the film, wishing he was under a spell and waiting for love's first kiss (or anything, he would think, dejectedly), and one day, he would wake up a human, a real human—free to feel whatever he wanted, do whatever he wanted, go wherever he wanted. That was Biff's greatest dream.

But in a very secret place, locked away, was what he really wished for—that he had never been created at all.

An Exceptionally Good Liar

"I can't believe we're still talking about this. I barely have enough breath to trek this high, let alone explain myself to you."

That was Selene. She and her brother were climbing a mountain in the Swiss Alps. There are very few things prettier than hiking the Alps early in the morning. The mountains are so high that they look blue, reflecting the light of the sky and making the scene seem almost unreal to Selene. She looked at the valleys below and saw little patches of greenery surrounding tiny blue lakes. Even the jagged, snowy mountains seemed warm on a day as clear as that one. The sun was beginning to peek over the edges of the mountains farthest east, making the clouds and sky run with color, the same way a broken egg yolk creeps onto everything on a breakfast plate. While Selene wanted to dismiss Anthony's annoying questions to enjoy the aforementioned scenery, which, she thought tersely, she definitely paid for, Anthony seemed to have other motivations.

"You're supposed to think of something while you hike. *I'm* thinking about how sincerely fucked it is that your ulterior motive for this leg of the trip is based on *Batman Begins* and a subreddit about secret societies!" That was Anthony, her brother. And he was not wrong.

Their guide, a friendly mountain man they met in town, was also silent, and seemed very, very awkward. His name was Klaus, and he had been up this mountain many times and knew the community very well. He spoke English, French, Italian, and Spanish, making him an easy guide to talk to.

The twins, after many years of saving and hard-work, decided to take a trip through Europe. Selene planned the trip meticulously, booking rooms in different cities, tracking multiple flights per city, and packing weeks in advance. They say twins complement each other but aren't necessarily similar—so Anthony let Selene do all the planning, and he packed at three am, four hours before their first flight. Most people know the twins to be opposites in this way; Selene an athletic intellectual and Anthony an intellectual athlete, with the former being the planner and the latter being the partier. The two were often at odds, but exclusively relied on each other.

Selene wasn't sure if there actually *was* a secret society up there, but she assumed she would like the trek anyway, and that there was at least a church community they could stay with. No harm in checking it out and seeing a cool church anyway, was all she thought at first, careful to avoid high expectations. Switzerland was the last leg of their trip. They had been all over France, Italy, Austria, Luxembourg, Belgium, and Germany. Both avid outdoors-people, they knew that climbing the Alps would be the climax of their trip, and so they saved the best for last. Selene had planned it that way, but with the aforementioned ulterior motives involving a secret society occupying a monastery in the Alps, at 5,500 meters above sea level. She lured Anthony in with the trekking and the monastery, two of his interests being hiking and medieval churches.

"Look, I just wanted to see if there was anything, and you wanted to do a trek anyway. And there *is* a monastery up here, so—just—relax—okay?" Selene stuttered, partly from fatigue and partly from nervousness. As this leg of the trip approached, she became more and more beguiled by the notion of a secret society; more and more intrigued by the world of possibility before her. She struggled to express the mix of excitement and apprehension within her, even to herself. The sun rose firmly in the east as the twins continued their trek from dawn and into the morning.

After some time, the trio made it to a lift created many years ago by the inhabitants of the area. The lift was made entirely of wood, large sturdy blocks boxing in about four people comfortably. The lift seemed just like an elevator but outdoors, with an ending that was difficult to see. The group had to travel in the coffin-like box for about two hours to reach the monastery. Selene stepped into the death box, attempting to hide her discomfort behind a guise of bravery— Anthony, on the other hand, walked into the lift so calmly, she assumed he was overcompensating. Her brother was a daredevil, but even Klaus looked solemn. As they all buckled their safety harnesses Klaus started the engine and the lift jerked up about four feet, then began to glide. They were finally on their way up.

Klaus, in an act of mercy, began to explain the history of the monastery, decreasing the tension between the siblings. "The monastery was built sometime in the 1600s and was always *Catholique* until around 1800, when mountain climbing became popular among the elites of Europe," Klaus spoke in English, but would often accidentally use French words for words that were similar in both languages. Selene knew several languages, as well, but Anthony only knew French and English, and his understanding of the former was high-school, at best. "So *naturellement* it became a *necessité* for the population to open their gates to travelers to practice their faith. In a way, at least. They knew they could not turn away people who had tried to climb the *montagne* and experience God in the way they themselves had, you know, because they were so high up and because they thought God could speak to them if they stood up high enough." Selene, naturally, knew all of this information. She had done her research on this monastery and the people living in it. Either Klaus didn't know the nuance of the story or he just didn't think she or Anthony knew. Selene had learned that they had had to open their gates because their supplies had begun to dwindle and the monks were starving. The farmers started to move away and so did the food, sparking rumors that members of the order were practicing cannibalism. The priests saw opportunity knocking, and they took it. Anthony listened intently, unaware of the finer points of the story.

"Are they still all Catholic?" Anthony queried, looking out of the lift into the atmosphere, slow, thin clouds parting as the lift passed through. Klaus grunted affirmatively, nodding slowly. Anthony was turned away, but Selene made eye contact with Klaus. She suspected that Klaus, honestly, couldn't tell if they were Catholic or something else. In one of the many sites and accounts Selene encountered, she found out that the monks wore habits, but no one ever really saw them praying or contemplating, or any of the other things religious people usually do. On Sundays everyone went into the church, but there wasn't singing or anything. She suspected that Klaus assumed the monastery was Catholic because it was one of the more austere sects of Christianity, but every Catholic mass she had been to had at least had singing.

The three descended into their own minds. Klaus intermittently checking on the machinery; Anthony's eyes glazed over as he continued to stare out of the lift; and Selene tried to imagine what the people would be like at the monastery.

When the lift finally reached its summit, Selene got her first look at the place she had been thinking about since finding that subreddit six years ago. The monastery was, in a word, impossible. It was impossible that a place 5,500 meters above sea level was the home of copious amounts of greenery, several buildings of varying size, and, not to mention, a church façade carved out of the mountain itself, standing eighteen feet high. It was a verifiable oasis, as if God had touched the monastery and shielded it from anything that would harm the impossible ecosystem that existed. She was amazed by the way it seemed lost in time, yet somehow timeless. Impossible, indeed, she thought.

By the elevator there was a lookout, presumably so tourists and residents alike could take in the incredible view. 5,500 meters above sea level leads to some pretty incredible sights, and when Selene and Anthony looked out from the elevator, they saw the full scope of the Alpen mountain range. The mountains were jagged, snowy, teeth-like, scale-like—all the descriptions that are clichés now to describe mountain ranges. From the gate house the juxtaposition was pronounced: the buildings were crawling with ivy and layered in old brick, a sign of the audacity of life against the cold, reptilian mountains. Selene smiled involuntarily, awestruck in her own way.

The twins and Klaus stepped out of the elevator and onto a platform that led into the Gate House, the gateway to the monastery. There, a man dressed in the robes of a priest shook their hands, and said something to Klaus in broken French, something Selene identified as "There are two rooms in the guest house if you want to take them there". The twins followed Klaus from the Gate House and onto the grounds of the monastery. Among the semi-circle of buildings was an infirmary on the west side, marked by an equal armed cross and an austere feeling, even from the outside. The vines of ivy and old, mismatched brick felt cold against the building.

The infirmary and monks' dormitory shared a garden filled with whatever basic foods the monks and their guests would eat. The dormitory, made with an equal amount of window and brick, looked somehow grimmer than any of the other buildings; it had no ivy growing on it, and out of the corner of her eye, Selene noticed lines of crosses stuck into the ground behind the grey building.

"There aren't any animals here," Anthony whispered to Selene as they walked behind Klaus towards the guest house.

"The monks don't eat meat," Klaus said over his shoulder to Anthony, "they don't even import it." They arrived at the house and Klaus held the door open for the two. Selene stopped walking when she noticed that Anthony had stopped short, admiring the four eighteen foot tall stone men that guarded the church. Selene hadn't noticed the statues before either, and thought it was funny that both of the twins could miss something so large.

"Cool, right?" Selene whispered creepily in Anthony's ear. Anthony disgustedly turned to Selene and shuddered jokingly.

"It is pretty cool. Incredible, really." Anthony turned back towards the guest house while Selene lingered.

"You coming?" Anthony projected. Selene turned on a dime and smiled.

"Yep! Be right there," she shouted, and walked towards her brother. They met with Klaus in the drawing room in the guest house, a comfortable building with ten two-bed bedrooms and warm wooden floors. As the three sat together in the drawing room, a priest named Zoran came to talk to them.

"Hi, Anthony and Selene. It is nice to meet you. We seldom get visitors and rarely are they so young!" Selene watched as Anthony's face shifted, reflecting a low-level suspicion she was familiar with.

Selene spoke up, "Well, both of us have always wanted to climb a mountain, and I had read about your monastery online, so it seemed coincidence or providence or something drew us here." Selene tried to be amicable while Anthony remained silent and guarded. Selene sensed no bad intentions from the man and lightly tapped Anthony's forearm to try and draw him out of whatever thoughts he was having.

"It seems so," replied the priest, nodding. He repeated the phrase with more vigor, surprising Selene, who had begun examining her nails. "It certainly seems so! Well, that's the way of the world, isn't it. Coincidence. Anyway. Klaus, I think rooms 34 and 35 are both free."

"Oh—we can share a room," Anthony said. Selene looked at him like he had just told their parents about the time they did cocaine in Mexico.

"Actually, if it's alright with you—" Selene started before Zoran interrupted.

"No, I insist. You two are too old to be sharing a room, anyway. The double beds are only if we get really busy."

Selene rolled her eyes at Anthony, "Thanks. We've been sharing a room all the way here just because we couldn't afford separate rooms. I really appreciate having my own bed." Selene, remembering she should be more gracious, quickly said, "But we don't really have money for a separate room and we really don't want to be taking up space if someone could—"

"Nonsense. Two rooms for two people. Klaus will show you. 34 and 35, Klaus. See you at dinner, children!" Zoran exited the room jauntily.

Selene looked around the room and felt a sort of familiarity. Like when you walk downtown and you smell what you instinctively know to be empanadas because your *abuela* used to make them, but you know those empanadas aren't your *abuela's* empanadas. That's exactly how Selene felt about this room. It reminded her of her parents' house before their dual death led to her and Anthony moving in with Marta and Alex, their godparents. Something about the airiness of the room reminded her of their old living room, her old happiness.

Selene was drawn out of her thought process when Anthony slapped his hands against his thighs, the universal signal for, "Let's get the fuck *moving*, people", and stood up. Klaus and Selene followed suit.

"Unfortunately, there are only stairs, but fortunately there are only three floors, so after the trek this should be a walk in cake," Klaus said, guiding the twins out of the parlor.

"Do you mean," Selene squinted, "a cake walk? Or, a walk in the park?" Her legs felt a bit like jelly after they had felt the sweet relief of sitting, and she relished the opportunity to sit again. The stairwell felt friendly, dotted with amateur paintings of various parts of the property, some more amateur than others.

"Ah!" Klaus exclaimed, "that's it. A cake walk. That's what I meant to say." He began muttering to himself about English and mentioned something about Australians having sex with spiders. Selene focused on making it up the stairs.

Anthony and Selene arrived at their rooms and agreed to meet up in about two hours, after they slept and showered.

Selene had planned to only nap for 52 minutes, two separate intervals of 26 minutes each, but she ended up sleeping for the whole two hours. She woke up with a start and jumped in the shower. Selene scrubbed her hair, brushed her teeth, and cleaned every nook and cranny as fast as she could, mostly on principle. She hated when other people were late and tried as often as she could to not be late herself. She also knew Anthony to be the kind of person to hold people to their principles.

Selene scratched at his door like a cat, a sort of joke and precaution the twins had. Anthony opened the door lazily, contrasting Selene's vomitus apology. "I'm *so* sorry I slept this long. You weren't waiting for me, were you?" She hastily stepped into his space and sat on his bed. "I can't believe how tired I was. I wanted to shower and shit."

"Literally shit?" Anthony joked, closing the door with a flick of the wrist.

"Metaphorically, shithead. Anyway. What do you want to do? Down to explore a bit?" Selene was tapping her foot, anxious to develop a plan.

"Well, I'm not sure. I don't want to work too hard, honestly, because I think I'm still getting used to this air pressure. How many times have your ears popped?"

Anthony began to cycle through a yoga flow, and Selene, lying, answered, "Like, 60 it feels like."

Selene had found a weekly class at a gym that simulated mountain air pressure. A lot of the people in the class were prepping for treks, just like her, and she had even made some friends there. The workouts were grueling, like CrossFit but Selene could never catch her breath because of the low air pressure. Every week she got stronger and stronger, and even though her recovery from each class felt like torture, by the time another one rolled around, she found the strength to go. She hadn't told Anthony about the classes and didn't really have a reason—she just didn't think to tell him. She also couldn't place why she lied to him when he asked about her ears popping, but something inside her told her that he wouldn't be receptive.

"But, like, what do you want to do? I don't want to miss out on stuff—"

"Dude, can you just relax? I didn't say I didn't want to do anything; I just also want to enjoy myself, and right now I'm enjoying this." Anthony continued through his flow.

"Ok, I—" Selene cut herself off. She had to constantly remind herself that she and her brother were different. She hated arguing with him but wanted him to take things seriously—take important things seriously, she corrected in her mind. He had strong opinions about post-credit scenes in movies and yet when their parents died, he showed up late for the funeral because he made plans to go see *Iron Man 3* with some sexual conquest. Selene got up and joined him in his *vinyasa*, pushing down the judgement lest it turn inward onto herself and her own choices, as it was wont to do.

"I definitely want to see the church," Selene prompted after a couple minutes of yoga.

"So, let's just go see that monolith of a church and hang out in the gardens," Anthony reached for the sky on an inhale, and on an exhale put his hands together and brought them to his chest. Selene followed suit. They agreed to meet in the hallway outside their rooms in about five minutes.

The "monolith" Anthony mentioned was the portico of the church, and, by extension, the church itself. The twins had read that the church *cella* was a natural cave that had formed in the mountain but with some adjustments. The congregation had dwindled so much in recent years that the tradition of expanding into the mountain every fifteen years stopped around 1947. The pediment was relatively plain compared to the four eighteen foot statues holding it. The statues were supposed to be depictions of the evangelists, Matthew, Mark, Luke, and John, while the pediment had a simple depiction of the last supper by an unknown artist dated *before* Da Vinci's interpretation and remarkably similar. Despite being hundreds of years old, the statues hadn't lost any of their definition due to human care, the eyes of each statue following your every movement. Selene examined the way the robes on the statues fell, and the small details of each piece; each fold, dimple, and detail adding to the overall larger-than-life affect. Selene noticed that the toes on Luke's right foot were raised, as if to scratch an itch between toes.

As the twins approached the portico they were impressed, but not exactly amazed. They had been to Rome, Paris, Barcelona—they knew impressive architecture and art. The statues were truly a marvel, but they worried that they represented the best the monastery had to offer. That being said, walking into the *cella* was a whole different story.

After years of expansion, the chapel was a sight to behold, as large as the Pantheon but substantially less decorated; It was easy to forget you were inside a mountain. The walls were white limestone carved with large depictions of the stations of the cross. The wooden pews formed a semi-circle around the altar and the twenty-foot, crucified Jesus gazing up into the nothingness. The podium, benches, and the altar itself all seemed to be carved from the same white limestone as the walls. There was no electricity in the place, only candles, giving it a haunting, movie-like ambience. Selene immediately pictured her own funeral happening within the church but tried her best to dismiss the thought. As they walked in, Selene did the sign of the cross with holy water she procured from a small basin near the entrance. Anthony abstained.

Walking around the chapel, Selene became very uncomfortable. She felt eyes constantly on her, and the crucifix felt graphic. If she stared at the nails in Jesus' hands and feet, she could almost see the blood move. She went to go light a candle by the altar for her parents, looking at her feet the whole time.

Selene could tell Anthony loved how eerily silent it was, how all the candles lit the place only just enough. Anthony loved medieval churches and their arbitrary sanctity. He had this quirk whenever he went into a church where he would have to touch every pew, and as he made his way through the place, touching every pew, Selene watched him to distract from her own persistent discomfort. He made his way over to Selene and put his arm around her.

"It's nice that you're lighting a candle for them. I think they would've really liked it here." Anthony hugged Selene tight. "I miss them all the time."

Selene nodded silently but wasn't really listening. Being there and being so close to an opportunity she had imagined for years made her feel anxious. She hugged her brother back and pushed the other thoughts away to keep him from suspecting she was still thinking about the possible secret society.

Anthony continued his mission to touch every pew while Selene meditated by the candles and tried not to make Anthony suspicious. She thought about her training and tried to release her expectations in case the secret society was just hearsay. After Anthony finished, the two walked out of the church and back into the light of day, which slowly began to fade. Klaus was hanging out on a wooden bench in the garden as they walked over.

"Hello, you two," he yawned, clearly smoking a roach. "I have more if you're interested. It's actually *rolled* into your tour fees," he laughed. The two weren't sure if he was serious but decided to partake anyway, the three squeezing onto the already uncomfortable bench. Selene had to give up some of her vices to steadily train, but marijuana was one she allowed herself to keep up, even in a lessened state; the twins shared more joints than they cared to tell anyone over the years. Klaus handed Selene a joint so she could light it and she immediately made fun of it.

"Did you roll this yourself? Because... it looks like shit," Selene joked. Anthony took it from her and examined it closely.

"It's not that bad Selene. Leave the guy alone." Anthony turned to Klaus, "I promise not *all* Canadians are joint-rolling snobs. This really isn't that bad."

"'That bad'? It's great. I don't know what you're talking about." Klaus snatched the joint back.

Anthony started to laugh. "Klaus, don't worry. Come on, let's smoke this. Relax, Selene really is just bothering you." Klaus reluctantly handed Anthony the joint and he lit it, nodding as he inhaled. "It's rolled a little loose, but it's all good. Still smokes well enough!" He passed it to Selene, who then passed it back to Klaus and so on.

After half a joint worth of miscellaneous conversation, Klaus posed a question to Selene and Anthony: Why do this trek?

"Well, Selene wanted to see if there was a secret society," Anthony spoke through an inhale, stretching his arms up as he did so. Selene shot him a look, annoyed.

"That's not why I'm here, that's just something I was curious about." Selene snatched the joint from Anthony, "Why don't you speak for yourself?"

Anthony, predictably, hadn't thought about why he had come on the trip, aside from: "Well, it seemed like a good way to celebrate an astounding five years of university." Klaus nodded understandingly, saying he had heard more disappointing answers.

"That's it? I don't know why I'm surprised, but, honestly? There's nothing else in your brain besides you wanting to party?" Selene scoffed and passed the joint back to Klaus.

"I also don't know why you're surprised. When have you ever known me to have deeper feelings about anything?" Anthony relayed this in such a matter-of-fact way that even Klaus was a little suspicious.

"You have deep feelings about Dijon mustard, why *wouldn't* you have deeper feelings about the trip of a lifetime? About *this* trip."

"I just wanted to see Europe. It has a lot of things I like, some of which I can't get at home. Partying after finishing my degree felt right, and up until this moment, I was enjoying doing it with one of my best friends." Anthony's defensiveness was a sure sign to Selene that he was hiding something, but she couldn't imagine what.

Seeming to sense the awkwardness Klaus exclaimed, "Dinner time! I'll take you to the food hall. We get to have dinner with the priests," almost falling over from making a large gesture with his hands. Selene and Anthony laughed despite themselves and wobbled up. The weed was stronger than they had expected, but not unmanageable or necessarily long-lasting.

As they walked from the garden to the dining hall, Klaus felt the need to brief the twins on dinner with the priests, which was strange enough to warrant some debriefing. "The priests eat in complete *silence*. The only sounds you hear are forks and spoons on plates and even that is kept to a *minimum*. They say it's so that they can meditate on the gifts that God has given them that day. Oh, and prayers before dinner last for about ten minutes. First you get served your vegetables and then you get served your *riz*, so you should eat them in that order. The monks will look at you funny if you try to eat them both at once." Klaus paused while Selene shot Anthony an unimpressed look. "Also, don't wear anything fancy to dinner," Klaus turned to Selene, "actually, if you have anything shapeless, you should probably wear that. The monks are sort of sexist." Selene scoffed.

"Of course they are. Let me guess, their wine tastes like vinegar and they also don't salt their vegetables?" Her brisk walk began to feel like a trudge.

Klaus looked at her sharply and then seemed to dismiss whatever thought he had, saying, "Good guess. They absolutely do *not* salt their vegetables. It's sort of astounding because there is actually quite a bit of flavor." Anthony talked absently about some of the oddest food they had in Paris, and Selene silently thanked him. Her mind had begun to wander, thinking about where a secret society could be hiding in this small community, and she became a bit dejected thinking about how impossible it would be in such a tight space. Part of her held on to the hope that perhaps she missed a clue, or after so many years of hiding they had just learned all the best ways to hide, besting even the greatest of detectives (Selene included herself amongst the best). Anthony rattled off more restaurants and what each of them ordered, his memory truly a marvel given how often he partied.

After about ten minutes of walking, they made it into the dining hall. The room felt warm, was furnished with long wooden tables, a large fireplace, and various pennants hanging from the walls and ceiling recognizing the myriad kings that had visited the hall. Anthony pointed to different pennants and told Selene which king it belonged to, most being Medieval. She wondered if it was seen as a great feat for kings to make their way up the mountain, and whether the newer looking pennants had just been mailed there. The twins followed Klaus to a small table at the end of the hall, clearly an addition.

"If you want to go back to your room to change, you can. Dinner won't be for a little while." Klaus and Anthony both sat down. Selene sat down with them.

"Aren't you going to go change?" Klaus asked incredulously.

Selene shrugged and mumbled about how she didn't have any looser fitting clothes, unwilling to conform to their sexism. Her sweatpants, flannel, and hoodie would have to suffice. Before Klaus could retort, Father Zoran sat down beside Selene.

"Great hoodie, Selene. Did you ever attend the University of Rome?" Selene began to tell the father about how she was gifted this sweater by their father before his death ten years ago, but Selene did attend the University of Rome for a semester.

"The older professors would always compliment me on it. I got my own while I was there, but this one is just better. You know?" Selene was happy for the opportunity to talk to the old man again; Selene was known to collect father figures, and she had immediately connected to this kind, energetic priest. Selene saw Anthony pat Klaus on the arm out of the corner of her eye and say something so him, while Klaus looked at Zoran suspiciously. Selene, too, was suspicious of Zoran sitting with them. Something in Klaus' face had illustrated to her that perhaps the priest didn't partake in dinner with the guests often, if at all. While Selene liked the man, she resolved to stay acutely aware of his movements, as well as the movements of the room.

As dinner progressed, Zoran spoke to the twins, curious as to what their lives were like, how they had liked university, how their adoptive parents treated them. Selene and Anthony, at the same time it seemed, pinpointed that Zoran's familiar accent was Serbian—their mother's family was Serbian, and they still talked to some of their cousins, and even met up with a few when they were in Paris. While the two barely spoke a word of Serbian, they were proud of their culture and asked Zoran questions about Serbian history they hadn't been able to learn from their mother. They found that the three of them had a lot in common besides a common heritage, including a love of tennis, impressionist art, and Italian cooking.

It happened in jump cuts for Selene. Something pulled her eye to the window—then a bullet that was so small at first, but then it was all she could see—she wondered if it would puncture her eyeball and if her eye would explode—then a realization: it was going to hit Zoran! Selene saw her hand reaching for a spoon. The bullet crawled closer. Her head turned to Zoran, her eyes saw where the bullet was going. She put the spoon up and blinked and when she opened her eyes—everything had sped up again.

About 16 different monks crowded around the table, while another 10 or more, including Klaus, left the room to, presumably, apprehend the gunman. Selene was looking around with just her eyes, her head unmoving. She saw

Anthony's mouth moving but couldn't hear him. Zoran was delegating to the men surrounding him in French, so unnervingly calm that he must've been in this situation before.

Selene began to examine the spoon clutched in her hand, contemplating how she was feeling. She remembered seeing the bullet, and felt her arm grab the spoon and hold it in the exact right spot, but her brain itself didn't seem to make the call. All Selene could do was smile knowing that all of her training had come to fruition, and she couldn't have imagined a better way to show everyone, all of these sexist monks, her brother, Klaus, and herself, just how incredibly strong she was. She was pulled from her reverie by Zoran, who patted her on the shoulder and smiled.

"Okay, *unuko*. Now, the real work begins."

Virago

What follows is an excerpt from a lost piece of ancient literature, by someone resembling Suetonius, The Life of Virago. *The text seems to have been a part of a larger text like* The Lives of the Caesars, *possibly titled* The Lives of Roman Women. *Sabina Matinia Virago is the only life remaining, and only in excerpt form.*

[1] The Matinii were well known for being fair and noble money lenders during the reign of Hadrian, but prior to this, they were known to be true arbiters of the republic and Rome, beginning in the days of the Republic with Sabinius Titus Matinius Primus, called so because he was the first of his name and launched the Matinii into power by distinguishing himself in Carthage all those years ago and marrying Caelia. They had three children, but Marcus died during the suppression of a rebellion in Africa. The other two, Martinia and S. T. Matinius Secundus married into prominent families, the Petronii and Flavii, respectively. Secundus was also a senator and was best known for walking throughout the capital and complimenting people's

entrances and archways, paying attention to the stones used by a builder. He was sometimes able to identify a builder by which brick he used. His mother, a Caelii by birth, was fond of pottery, and Secundus would frequently stop in storefronts to purchase her a bowl or a trinket of some sort that caught his eye. Caelia would always say that a beautiful, earthen bowl begged to be filled with beautiful sacrifices to the gods.

[2] The family fell into disrepute after an *iniuria* incurred by the grandson of Secundus and a woman of a noble family, Statilia. The Statilii maintained that Gallus Ttius Matinius the Younger defiled Statilia to prevent her from becoming a Vestal Virgin. Gallus the Younger claimed that he had no reason to think Statilia was to become a Vestal Virgin, stating that Statilia was promised to him and he was simply overzealous. The ordeal was brought to court and is well documented. To this day no one admits any fault. In the end, Gallus was found guilty and offered to be exiled to prevent his brother, Sextus Titus, from paying an overly large fine. Sextus, already married to Hortensia, distanced himself from his brother by signing documents as only Sextus Titus. Paulina, the mother of Gallus and Sextus, was said to have followed her son into exile, but only because she miraculously went missing after the ordeal.

[3] Despite all the problems caused by Gallus' indiscretion, Sextus was able to secure for his son a marriage into the Marullinii family, with Sabinus Titus Matinius Aquila marrying Aelia Marullinia, daughter of Aelius Hadrianus. Aelia was the most beautiful of her sisters, although the youngest. The story goes that Sabinus Aquila was fond of walking in the evenings around the capital and sneaking into gardens to steal fruits, vegetables, and flowers. Though his nickname, Aquila, came from his uncanny ability to see enemies on the battlefield from almost two miles away, it was joked that he was also very good at seeing which gardens had the best fruit. One night, feeling brave, he climbed a tree

adjacent to the Marullinii garden complex—or so he thought. The tree he climbed led directly to Aelia's balcony. Instead of screaming or calling for help, she told him that if he could answer a riddle she posed, not only would she not tell anyone about the encounter, or what she knew his true mission was, but she would marry him. The riddle is lost to time, but the two were married a month later, and after much deliberation between the two families.

[4] Sabinus Titus Matinius Primus was the first of the family to truly make a name for himself, becoming a senator due to a strange sequence of events. Everyone knows that first one must be a magistrate to be a senator, and Sabinus Primus, it is said, was elected to the magistracy by Jupiter himself. The Matinii were a strong but little-known patrician family before Sabinus. They had made their fortune in agriculture, owning several properties outside of Rome through various marriages. They had been Romans since the beginning, but still they remained obscure. The people of Rome chose Sabinus Primus because he seemed to have Rome's best interests at heart. He ensured bread was provided to soldiers during their training, made himself well known throughout the city, and was the patron of many an artist. He was the one who paid for the famed statue of Romulus and Remus, since destroyed.

[5] After serving his time as magistrate, the time came for Sabinus to be chosen from the many to be a senator. Sabinus was born with the lightest hair and continued to have light hair until he died. Some compared him to Apollo for how regal and celestial he looked. One night, it is said, the two consuls, L. Domitius Ahenobarbus and Ap. Claudius Pulcher, both had the same dream, and that was of a light-haired man donning a senator's robes and then giving these robes to a man who seemed to be his son, and so forth and so forth. Everyone knows that most magistrates become senators, but after this tandem dream the two consuls had no choice but to

bestow unto Sabinus the title of Senator, and after his death his son pursued politics and so on and so forth.

[6] Sabinus Aquila, due to his willingness to contribute to Roman well-being, earned the offices of monetalis and one of his former servants, acquired as a gift, became treasurer of the Augusta. Sabinus Aquila had two sons and a daughter with Aelia, the eldest being Sabinus, the middling being Gallus Canus, so called because his hair began growing grey early in his life, and the daughter being Aelia Minor. Aelia was chosen to become a Vestal Virgin and was much adored by her family for this. Both Sabinus and Gallus Canus, in their own times, would be chosen to be magistrates and then senators, Gallus Canus in his mid-life due to his charismatic personality and level headedness, and Sabinus, for opposing reasons. Where Gallus Canus was calm, Sabinus was fiery, and though the two rarely saw eye-to-eye, truly they provided lively entertainment for the Senate. Gallus Canus married Fabiana Aurelia, not known for her beauty but rather for her deep understanding of the cosmos and ability to read the entrails (despite never having studied them), and Sabinus married Lucia Caedicia, known best for her beautiful murals, some of which can be seen on houses throughout the capital. Her father was her greatest patron.

[7] Gallus Canus was the father of Virago, and, as she was his only child who lived past her name day, he treated her as equal to any son and trained her in the arts of war. Fabiana had had a troubled pregnancy, and all the midwives were sure that either her or the child would not survive the birth. Fabiana dreamt almost every night of a black she-wolf coming into her room and tearing her open to get to the baby, and everyone worried that this was a sure indication of death. On the day of her birth, all present waited with heavy hearts on the results of the difficult pregnancy. As Fabiana was giving birth, the same she-wolf from her dream came into the room and simply watched. When it came time to

cut the cord connecting Fabiana and Virago, the she-wolf herself stepped in and separated the two. Everyone sat in awe as the wolf cleaned the child and then left the room. When everyone came to their senses, they saw that Virago had a full head of black hair. She was born Sabina Matinia on the kalends of March during the consulship of Sex. Attius Suburanus Aemilianus II and M. Asinius Marcellus at the Matinius family home on Via Quirinalis.

[8] Virago got her cognomen when she was a child. She was known to get into fights with the boy children of elites, frequently coming home with bruises and getting called cruel names. She would keep her hair in two long braids on the side of her head at the insistence of one of her nurses, and boys would tug them and call her Longa. One day when she was eight years old, she became especially sick of this name, cut off her long braids, and began to wear her hair short. Many people mistook her for a boy after that, and so they began to call her Virago. This was also practical, as with short hair she greatly resembled her cousin Sabinus the Younger.

[9] From the time she was very young she was a proficient athlete. She often raced her male peers around their school near the Palatine. In her sixteenth year she participated in a decathlon held in the capital where she bested all the men who participated. She came to participate in the decathlon by posing as her cousin, Sabinus the Younger, who was slightly younger than her and gained much fame later for battles in Gaul. Because Virago was slight in appearance and strong, she excelled at the decathlon, and when she revealed herself to the participants, and to the emperor himself, who was inconspicuously watching within the crowds, a star sailed through the sky like Diana's own arrow. The haruspices present all agreed that her victory was a sign from the goddess herself.

[10] Virago was known best for her war contributions, but she was also known throughout the kingdom for her physical

prowess in general. Alongside her cousin, Sabinus, she fought as well as any man, and was arguably more bloodthirsty. She helped quell the revolts in Judea in her adulthood but always fought and supported the Empire in any battle the Emperor asked her to participate in. On the feast day of Jupiter, during the customary gladiator battle, she was asked personally by the emperor to be his champion and beat four out of the seven gladiators she was paired with, the other three withdrawing upon seeing her rip out the fourth man's throat after he had asked if her sword was too heavy for her—it was her custom to hold her sword in both hands for a more aggressive attack, but he did not expect such a stance from such a slight girl, and took it as weakness. That man, if you recall, was known as a serial rapist.

[11] There is another popular story involving Virago that many still tell. She was an admirer of home gardens, like her grandfather, Sabinus Aquila, and would, too, sneak into gardens at night. One night, when she was scaling a high wall, she happened upon two men in cloaks speaking in the garden of Sextus Catullus. She immediately recognized them as Sextus Catullus the younger and his friend, Marcus Fundanus, and the two were stealthily attempting to plot the emperor's demise. Having a good relationship with the emperor, Virago waited until the morning *salutatio* to inform the emperor, tastefully and privately, that the two seemed to be plotting against him. The emperor immediately sent for these men and, after Virago identified them a second time, questioned them until they eventually relented and exposed their whole plot. Virago was a hero in the emperor's eyes, though no one knew of her good deed besides him and her family.

[12] Sabina Virago, like her aunt, remained a virgin for all her days. She had no desire to marry and was too involved in the art of war to commit to a husband. And certainly, no men desired to marry her because she was not bestowed with

any of the gifts a woman should have in order to be a suitable match. She was pretty, indeed, but she was not submissive, nor a maternal type, nor was she good at flower arranging, or painting. She was, though, very well suited to be a general, having a level head, like her father, and a substantial amount of military experience. She tried many a time to place a bid for magistracy, citing her military experience and familial history, but to no avail...

Undercover

M: My name is Mary F[redacted]. I am currently working undercover for CSIS. This is an official recounting of my participation in disposing of a body. A fellow sex worker came to me and asked for my help in disposing of said body. I am making this statement such that the body can be recovered from lock up for the family to deal with and to clear up any allegations of foul play. I am of the opinion that no actions should be taken at this time.

H: My name is Harry C[redacted]. I am Mary's field officer, and I am here to conduct this interview and get the details of the case. Start from the beginning. How the fuck did you even get into this situation?

M: I don't—Harry, where—you know the whole story from the beginning! What do you want—

H: Mary, you know what I mean. From the beginning of this fucking ordeal—

M: Well, Michael is a good kid—he's bi and twink-y so he's popular with women and men. The men pay more, but the women aren't as rough. He's always taking these men who look sleazy, so I told him that I would help him out if he ever needed anything—

H: Jesus Christ, Mary—

M: Harry, just let me fucking talk. This isn't even that bad of a fuck-up. You were in Sarajevo—

H: (sighing) We're not talking about me, Mary. Just get to the story.

M: Alright, I get it, I'm a bleeding heart. He's—Michael, he's just so young. He's trying his best. The old guy he was (pause) servicing just collapsed on top of him. It could've happened to me, too, Harry.

H: Don't tell me that, Mary.

M: What, do you not want to hear that? Is that something you don't want to hear?

H: Keep this story the fuck moving, Mary.

M: You're unbelievable, Harry.

H: Keep. The. Story. Moving.

M: Right after it happened, Michael called me. He was panicking. He asked me to drive over to the guy's place in Midtown.

H: How'd you get to Midtown?

M: I grabbed my car. I went home first. I didn't think it would be a good idea to take public transit.

H: (sighing)

M: I can't—(groans). So, I drive to Midtown, park my car, go up to the house. I call Michael to let me in and he does. I'm obviously calm, he notices, and asks me how I could possibly be so calm. I tell him honestly that it's not my first rodeo and that I've seen a dead body before. (pause) Whatever, Harry. I wasn't really thinking about it and it wasn't my priority to continue being dishonest.

H: Whatever.

M: We go upstairs—

H: The dead bodies are always upstairs.

M: (snickering) A painful coincidence. I felt a little for the medics after having to carry that body.

H: Certainly not too much sympathy—

M: Are you serious—

H: You're incapable of human emotion—

M: Get over it, Harry—

H: Well, except the emotions you have for this Michael twink—

M: Hey! Don't say that fucking word!

H: What, did "twink" suddenly become a slur? After you said it? What a surprise.

M: We've been over this, Harry. When you said twink just now, you said it in such a negative way. You made it into a slur. Stop trying to use that argument. (pause) I don't want to be here, either, Harry.

H: Get on with it then.

M: I—Okay, so I tell him it isn't my first rodeo. I ask him what time he thinks this all happened, and he says he called me right away so about an hour before I got there. It dawns on me that perhaps the guy had a heart attack, and maybe we can just make it look like he was at home and something just happened. He was an old man, so it's not out of the realm of reason that he might have just, you know, had a heart attack—

H: We found him on the toilet, Mary.

M: That was our final choice. We had a pretty lengthy conversation about what the best option was. We knew we had to move him quickly though.

H: What made you trust this guy implicitly? What made you think that he didn't do anything? How could you have ruled out foul play so quickly?

M: Well, Harry, I'm no idiot. I sent the kid out for a smoke, told him to calm down, and that I would get the body cleaned up—get rid of his fingerprints, whatever. That kind of BS. I checked for track marks everywhere, even between the toes, I checked his mouth to see if he had been poisoned—which, yes, Harry, isn't perfect, but I did my best.

H: You really—

M: My hunch ended up being right, anyway. I got a copy of the tox report, same as you, and there was nothing wrong. He literally had a heart attack while having sex. It's not unheard of, Harry.

H: It's—it's extremely rare though.

M: It's like a 1 in 100 chance for men actually.

H: What is this, a PSA?

M: (audible sigh) If the toilet was such a poor choice, what would you have done, Harry?

H: I would've just called the cops and been honest.

M: If you were a prostitute?

H: Well, he could—

M: Are you recommending a prostitute lie to the police?

H: Not lie per se, just bend the truth?

M: I thought we could've put him in the shower with it running, just to rake up his water bill.

H: (scoffing) That's horrible!

M: I'm not a fan of rich people, generally. But, come on, the toilet was perfect. It also gives the family the opportunity to keep up appearances, in a way. Or, rather, I guess, lets them suspend their disbelief about him for a little longer if they didn't know he was frequently hiring male prostitutes.

H: I think, if I'm really racking my brain (pause) I would have just left him in the bed but, like, made it look like he was sleeping.

M: Yeah, that would've probably been the easiest solution. I got it into my head though that Michael might've gotten prints somewhere on his back or something and I got paranoid. Like, what if I hadn't handed in my report on time yada yada. I don't know, the bathroom kind of just made sense. We were able to wrestle him into the shower and clean him up a bit and still get him onto the toilet for his bowel evac.

H: Do you remember that Russian guy? We put him—

M: Oh my gosh, yes! We had to carry him into his fucking car! That was horrible.

H: I took all the weight. You pretty much just held his feet—

M: Whatever. I pulled my weight. I also did all the clean up!

H: But nothing was worse than Sarajevo.

M: I only heard stories, but, yeah. Sounds like it was a shit time.

H: Horrible. So much clean up and fixing. You know, when I look back at it, and sometimes I do, none of it even makes sense. We weren't even supposed to be there that day; it was actually a total fucking accident. It makes me paranoid to think that maybe everything was orchestrated from the beginning—

M: Oh, god. That's horrible.

H: Yeah. Just thinking about it makes me tired.

M: Well, this wasn't that bad, at least not on a scale of 1 to Sarajevo.

H: (laughs) It actually sounds like it was quite a debacle though.

M: At least you can laugh about it now. I'm glad you've calmed down. You were actually fucking nuts for the last couple days.

H: Well, I guess I'm just realizing everything went—

M: I think that if I could've done anything differently though, I would've just left him in the bed—

H: What are you doing with your hands?

M: Instead of even moving him.

M: What're you doing?

H: What do you mean?

M: Harry, knock it off! (whispering)

H: It's off—

M: The recorder is never off with you, Harry. (sigh) Are we done here? I have an appointment soon.

H: Jesus, Mary, I don't want to hear that. Plus, they have nothing—

M: I don't really care. Don't be an idiot. Shut up, don't say anything about this to anyone, and let me leave.

H: Fine.

M: (sounds of chair moving) Fine. Don't say a fucking word, Harry. He was a piece of shit, and now he's dead, but that's all just coincidence. Right?

H: Yes.

M: I'll see you when I see you. Did you put in my transfer papers?

H: Yes. McGuinness will contact you with your new RO.

M: Good. (pause) Later, Harry.

H: Later.

Seven Minutes in Heaven

"Oh, a suicide? She's only going to be in one place, bud," She said, looking at Her clipboard intently.

Paul swallowed hard, "Hell?" he whispered, desperately, anxiously.

"Oh, no. God, no. Hell doesn't exist. She's in Rehab. Well, the only Rehab—the one we house in our Temple. Come with me." She took his hand and they were transported to a beautiful temple in the mountains of what he believed to be an Asian country; but he didn't think it was a temple that denoted any religion in particular. Paul marveled at the beauty of the temple for only a moment before they were floating into the foyer. She let go of his hand and began to explain why they were there.

"With suicides, we put them in Rehab for 100 years. Here they have access to therapists, philosophers, religious figures—anyone and anything that will put them in a healthier state of mind so that they can be safely reincarnated. It's supposed to lessen the chance of their next soul-slash-body repeating history, so to speak, but we haven't seen any distinct correlation between the two. We do the same thing for murderers and rapists et cetera, but they're all in different facilities and for a different number of years. And absolutely not for the same reasons." She was flipping through Her papers while they floated along. As they floated through the rooms, a tactic Paul guessed was so She had more time to look through the papers, he watched the countless number of people in this temple doing their own interpretation of what he described as exercise. Some were doing yoga in a round and colorful room, others seemed to be singing while sitting in a circle; he was interested in this place but had a feeling he couldn't stay too long.

Paul turned to Her and said, "So we *do* get reincarnated. When will I go to my next body? When I finish my three wishes?" Before he even asked, he knew this was the case. He was still trying to think of his other two wishes, but he knew seeing Linda again was a good first choice.

"Yup. After your wishes are up. You go into the first available body—the time conversion is, like, every hour you spend here is about a millisecond on Earth, so what they say about reincarnation is sort of true. Everyone should get some sort of reward, right?" She wasn't even looking up from Her clipboard and they still made it through all the doorways.

"How do you decide who goes into rehab besides people who died from suicide or mental illness? I mean I understand rapists and murderers and I guess suicides when you explain it, but, like, pedophiles then, right? They must go to rehab? But then what about, I don't know, gay people? That's a thing in the Bible you're not supposed to do."

She scoffed, "I told you people get reincarnated, and you still think we listen to the Bible up here?"

"Well, I-I mean... yeah? Uh, yes?"

"No," She stated, "it's not the Bible we listen to up here. It's also not the Quran, or the Sutras, or the Talmud. Unfortunately, I guess, for everyone who thought it was."

Confused, Paul asked, "So, you just *let* people fight religious wars for nothing? Knowing that none of them were right?"

"Everyone was sort of right, okay? No one was *completely* wrong." Paul watched Her rub Her thumb and forefinger together, what he assumed was a nervous tick. "Look, everyone voted, and everyone wanted free will. What were we supposed to do?" Paul could see Her brow furrow in frustration and Her eyes drop to Her papers. "As it was, we had to start from scratch. That was awful." She stopped shuffling papers, obviously deep in thought. Paul, though not tactful in life, could sense that he had hit a nerve. He decided to pivot slightly.

"So, what stage of the cycle does a soul actually go into the body? In Hinduism I think they believe—"

She clipped Her papers to Her clipboard and flipped onto Her back floating in the air the same way someone might leisurely float along the water. "Well, it's a little complex. The karma thing is true, but we're much more lenient than you think. We fully embrace the fact that people are people, so unless you do something worth note, i.e., mass murder, then we step in."

The temple seemed to stretch on forever, and as they passed crowds and crowds of people, Paul began to feel sad thinking of all the people who had died from suicide. Paul had known someone in high school who later died from suicide. Paul hadn't really kept up with him, but he had heard about the death through the grapevine. He wondered if he would recognize him if the opportunity arose.

"I know it seemed like I equated the two, murder and suicide, but we really don't. We don't exactly torture murderers or anything, but we don't treat them the same way we treat people who died from suicide," She said, drawing Paul out of his thoughts. "Suicide falls within the same tree as mental illness in general." She adjusted Herself so She was sitting crossed-legged instead of lying down and began to draw a chart.

"We have this temple, here, and a bunch of other adjacent temples. In them are trillions of people who passed away from different mental illness-related things. Unfortunately, a lot of them die from suicide."

"Free will?" Paul posited.

"Free will." She shrugged. "Free will. My hands are tired. Tied, rather, but also tired. Anyway, most mental illness we try to help. DID, Depression, there are different wings for every type of ailment and different ways to assist all the people who pass on, based on what people need. Some just need to face the dragon, some need to go on a quest first. Suicide, though, is a horse of a different color."

Paul saw Her look down at the people in the Temple, people walking through hallways, saying hello to others, crying, laughing, meditating, eating. She sighed. "As often as I come here, it doesn't get easier. Do you know how much I wish I could just play God like they say in the movies? End all of the wars, the sadness, the murder—the trauma?" She stopped talking abruptly and shook Her head.

"You're really getting me worked up, Paul. I'm often pretty level-headed. But some people... you know, I think it's working with Humans. I haven't worked with Humans in so long. You're just not developed enough as a race to really understand the complexity yet."

"What? Who do you normally work with?"

Before he could say anything else, She cut him off.

"Linda is in the Buddhist wing right now. It's my understanding that she bounces around the temple, but mostly she helps out in the Children's Wing." His first thought was, 'Same old Linda', and his second thought was, 'I can't believe children die from suicide'. His mood dampened imagining the parents, and imagining something happening to his own children, something that he hadn't noticed. They began their slow descent into the Temple and walked towards what he assumed was the Buddhist wing.

"Do you have something you're going to say to her?" She asked absently, holding Her clipboard behind Her back.

"What?"

"You know, 50 years of sadness balled into one highly-produced sentence? You've never thought about what you would say if you saw her again?"

Paul thought for a moment. "Well, I always imagined it would be something like this actually."

"Really?" She remarked, obviously surprised.

"Not in a temple or anything, nothing this specific. No, I mean, I just imagined it would be after I died and that I would get to see her. I sometimes thought of what I would say—50 years of sadness in one sentence, as you said—but nothing ever felt right. I still don't know what I'll say. I can barely comprehend that I'll be seeing her again." Paul hadn't thought that before but saying it aloud he knew it was true. How could he fathom confronting what was, in his opinion, the worst thing to ever happen to him? He positioned Linda's death at the focal point of his life, the focal point of his issues. All his abandonment issues, a mistrust of his parents that lasted until their deaths, commitment issues. He had done years of therapy and knew that it was wrong to put this much pressure on one event, but he found it easier to do—because then all he had to do was confront that event right? And the issues would go away? Soon he was standing in a large open space where scores of people were meditating.

"They'll be done soon," She whispered. "Guided meditation is very popular but kind of short. We get complaints all the time, but it's up to the guru, really."

Paul had resolved to stand silently until She spoke. "She died when you were pretty young, right?" She asked Paul, rubbing her thumb and forefinger together again.

"Well, pretty young, yeah. I was 15 and she was 20."

"At least you have good memories of her, then." Paul decided to engage in conversation, hoping it would relax him a bit.

"Yeah. Actually," he scoffed, "most of my fondest memories of her I have from times we walked home together. She was picking me up from school for as long as I can remember." Paul fell into memories and was able to still recall the feeling of flying he would get when Linda would pick him up and spin him around. This stopped as soon as even Linda became too cool to have fun with her younger brother in public but would have resumed if she had been able to pick him up as they grew older. He laughed a bit to himself.

"What's so funny?" She mumbled, having returned to browsing papers.

"Well, there was this one time—" but She cut him off.

"Hold that thought. They seem to be letting out earlier than expected—"

As people started getting up, he began to look for Linda, but couldn't find her. He immediately became worried, flashing back to the night when he lost her euphemistically and literally and, as if possessed, he cupped his mouth with his hands and hissed, "Linda!" About 50 people turned around, and another 40 or so shushed him loudly, a reaction which always bothered him. Despite his frustration, he mumbled a 'sorry' and shrank. He turned to Her and asked, "Where is she? What do I do?"

She smiled warmly and replied, "Just wait. She knows you're here. She'll be along in a second." He felt annoyed, elated, and frightened at the same time. He tried to focus on his breathing the way his therapist had taught him but found he couldn't inhale or exhale completely without shaking. He closed his eyes and inhaled for eight seconds, held his breath for four, and exhaled for seven, hoping the diverted focus would help relax him. He closed his eyes, and after eight deep inhales, She whispered, "She's here," and he felt his heart begin to race.

Linda didn't look a day over 20, and you wouldn't know she had been dying of cancer unless you noticed her bald head; he mused that it was probably hard not to notice, especially if one was prone to looking people in the eye when speaking to them. She was wearing skinny blue jeans and a band t-shirt, a typical look for her. Linda had almond eyes that were always smiling and a bevy of freckles on her nose and arms. One of the physical traits he remembered most ardently was her noticeable diastema and he was reminded of the way she used to stick straws in it and poke Paul when he was turned away. He watched as her smile grew and tears began to fall from her eyes. He took two large steps and collided with her, almost knocking her over and causing both of them to start laughing progressively louder, as if competing to see who could laugh the loudest and the strangest. After a moment, he picked her up and spun her around, ending the game but continuing to laugh.

Before Paul could feel embarrassed at the people watching them, the three of them were transported to what he presumed to be a private room in the building where they could talk in peace. The room was round and bright with seating sunken into the floor. In the middle was a table with incense burning on it. Paul put Linda down and looked at her. They stopped laughing and she smiled sadly, turning away to walk towards the sunken-in seating. Paul followed, but She held back. He turned to look at Her.

"Go ahead. I'm here."

He nodded solemnly and continued walking, feeling his feet get heavier with every step. A lifetime of anger, grief, sadness, loneliness, and longing flooded into him as he sat down, and the only thing he could do to quell it in any way was put his head between his knees. He felt transported back to that day in the hospital, old enough to know what was going on, too young to rationalize it, to feel anything but overwhelmed. He felt a hand on his back, which made him break out into full sobs.

He felt something light interact with his hair. It felt like a feather, 'but why would it be a feather?' he thought. He lifted his head and met eyes with a box of tissues, one peeking out and now touching his nose.

"If you've got an issue," Linda said, in a terrible impersonation of Michael Caine, "Here's a tissue!"

Linda began to laugh and then Paul, after a moment of sheer shock, began to laugh, too. Hysterically. The two of them proceeded to quote *Austin Powers*, which morphed into making *Harry Potter* references (for whatever reason) and again into references to *To Wong Fu, Thanks for Everything, Julie Newmar*. Paul let himself go, drifting in and out of memory and present, laughing more than he had allowed himself to after his divorce. He joked with Linda like she hadn't died when he was 15 and, realizing this, he stopped himself abruptly.

"I think it's a little preposterous, you know, if this afterlife isn't so strict on Biblical rules, that she's even here," Paul turned to Her, who didn't realize to whom he was talking.

"Me?" She questioned.

"Yes," he said, "you."

The air got heavy as Paul watched Her look at Linda, confused, "Paul, I didn't—"

"She was in pain—she was *dying*. She was in pain and couldn't take *cancer* anymore which, *you* let her get—does that mean nothing? She was a vibrant, intelligent woman, and—she could have been the *soul* animating the *person* who, I don't know, creates—a—something to—get people to the moon in, like, an airplane—or that lady that *cured* cancer—or something!" Paul's mind raced, and his breathing got heavy.

"Hey, man, look—" She stuttered, but before Paul could reply, he felt Linda's hand grip his arm in a way that read clearly to Paul as 'relax'.

"I got this. I'm sorry." Linda looked at Her pleadingly. "Can we have a moment alone?" She squinted at Linda and shrugged.

"Yeah, no worries. Not a ton of time left on this one though." She walked through the door.

And then walked back in, "You know what, I'm going to knock on the door twice— three—no, okay, four times for the last hour you have. Like, once every 15 minutes until the end. Then I'll knock to signify that the hour is done, and you have a 10-minute grace period before I come in and get you."

Linda shot a look of confusion at Paul, who shot her a look back, pursing his bottom lip and looking off to the side.

"I mean, yeah, I think that's fair," Linda said.

"Okay. Yeah. Anyway, I'll be out here. Remember, one knock equals one hour, and then subsequent knocks—"

"Yeah—yes, for sure. Okay. Great!" Linda replied, and She left the room.

Linda let go of Paul's arm, and clasped her hands in her lap.

"I—Paul, it isn't what—I'm not—Jesus, I can't believe this." Linda threw her hands in the air and let them fall into her lap. Paul sensed frustration.

"I saw *Mom*—I had to *say* this to my own *mother* and somehow this is harder. Telling you is harder." Paul began to think of his mother's death and how, if he had known she would see Linda, he might've tried to connect with her a little more before she died.

"Paul—my god, 60 years and I still can't say it. I still can't say it to you." She took a deep breath in. Paul was beginning to think the worst of his sister.

"I *wasn't* in pain. I wasn't even *dying* anymore. Of, like, *cancer* at least."

Paul felt, in this moment, like he was being told about Linda's death a second time. He was in tenth grade the day he found out she died. He was in English class, and they were learning about onomatopoeia. He remembered his principal speaking over the PA in his classroom, asking Paul to come to the office. As he walked the 47 steps from his classroom to the office, he prepared himself to hear about Linda. He had anticipated the eventuality that she would go and equipped himself with all the necessary items to journey through grief. But, ultimately, nothing he did or said or asked her before she died would have helped. He heard his mom say it and kept repeating the words in his head. He repeated the words until they were just sounds. Creating that pattern was the only thing that got him out of the school without crying.

Once, when he was taking a shrink's advice on how to deal with her death, he decided to write poetry. The only, and best, thing he ever wrote was: 'death onomatopoeia equals silence' and convinced himself that expanding on it would only ruin it.

Words poured out of Linda's mouth, and Paul absorbed none of them. How do you begin to comprehend the shattering of a belief you held for most of your life? How do you go from feeling immense sadness to immense anger without hurting people in between? And then how do you let go of the anger when you're in a time crunch? Paul dug his fingernails into his thighs, trying to focus on anything so he could start listening to Linda, trying to understand her, trying to use his equipment, but Paul gave in.

"How—so, you weren't dying, but—so you *decided*? You decided to die?"

Paul saw Linda reach for his hands in slow motion and pulled them away as fast as he could.

"You didn't even leave a note? You couldn't—"

"No, I couldn't, Paul!" Linda cried. Paul immediately became disgusted with himself.

"I spent my whole life—"

"Paul, I—"

"My whole life *defending*—"

"I'm still—"

"You're pathetic—"

"Paul, stop, you don't—"

A knock on the door caused them both to stop and turn their heads in horror.

Paul began to think about how his whole life culminated in this moment. The only thing he really asked of the afterlife was that it reunite the two of them so he could finally forgive her. The thought that she hadn't died to escape from pain had crossed his mind, but he ultimately thought that that was impossible. It was the reason he always reverted to based on his interpretation of his sister. She was cool, and fun, and happy, and kind, and cancer had taken her will to live—physical, bodily pain had caused her to nobly end her life. He spent so long working through that idea that he never considered another reason. Truthfully, every other reason was harder to accept.

Looking at her all he felt was immense pressure to forgive her, because if he didn't, what kind of person would he be? They had less than an hour together before he would forget her, how could he not just bury the hatchet? He thought this through clenched teeth, realizing that he was also angrier than he had allowed himself to be after the divorce.

Paul's anger became more focused, and he began to hear what Linda was saying.

"The cancer was in remission, but I was so tired. I was athletic, I was gorgeous, I had friends—none of them came to visit me because they couldn't handle the fact that I was sick, and I couldn't get out of bed—I couldn't even lift my notebook some days. And mom—oh, god, you remember mom—she blamed herself, threw out every soap and shampoo and non-natural product in the house. She blamed dad until she died, she told me when I saw her. I became so sad—I was depressed. I had lost everything and I believed, sincerely, that everything was my fault and that everyone hated me—I felt pathetic, and even though the cancer was in remission—I-I-I just thought that it would happen again, and that everything would get worse—" They heard another knock on the door.

Paul began to comprehend more and more of what she was saying.

"I had been in the hospital for 18 days and was missing Nan's funeral. You were all there at the funeral home, and I was in bed. I hadn't even been able to get up to fucking *pee*, and a doctor came in—the older lady, the no-nonsense one—and she asked me where you all were, and I told her and started to *cry* and I felt like such a terrible person, and then she told me about the remission and I couldn't even do anything. I felt, like, powerless, and just—it couldn't be true. This had to end, you know? I obsessed over the fact that it would come back, it was just in remission. I couldn't— I can't believe that after years of therapy, meditation, everything, this feeling is still inside of me—" She started to cry, and Paul's eyes widened as he tried to hold back tears himself.

Years in therapy hadn't prepared Paul for seeing his dead sister crying in the afterlife. He felt the third knock reverberate in his eardrums. He tried to think about how he was feeling. Seeing her cry had diminished his anger considerably. He was transitioning into guilt. He felt as though he had made her cry and had ruined what could have been a therapeutic moment for both of them. Paul tried to move on, to actively put away his sadness and hurt to make the best of the last few moments they had together. He breathed in deeply and forced himself to talk to her.

"You were probably depressed before the cancer, don't you think?" Paul said, more biting than he wanted it to be.

Linda sighed, having been holding her breath to try and stop the sobs. "I guess so. I didn't know what life was like without it until I died. I'm still trying to work through it all. Seeing mom helped. And so did shedding the belief that it was something I could fight alone. I wish—" Linda started sobbing again and said tersely, "Seeing you feels like starting all over."

Paul looked at his watch. Ten more minutes with a ten-minute grace period. They needed to move on because he was set to be reincarnated and he still had some wishes to cash in. He thought again about how her death was his cornerstone—something he had never gotten over in life. He thought about the next person whose body he would inhabit—or, whatever, he thought—and thought he *owed* it to that person to be better.

He ran to the door as quickly as possible and flung it open. He looked around for Her and saw Her sitting cross-legged in a courtyard opposite the room. He hadn't expected the door to lead outside.

He waved at Her and jogged to Her, his joints burning from the effort. He briefly wondered how old he was if Linda still looked 20 but dismissed it. "I want—I want my next wish to—be more—time," he panted with his hands on his knees.

Before She could say anything, a hand touched Paul's shoulder.

"Paul, that's not how this works. You can't just game God."

Paul tipped backwards from his folded position and fell, tailbone first, onto the grass. He let his back flatten and his limbs stretch out before shading his eyes with his forearm and letting tears flow.

He felt someone sit down beside him. "You were so young, Paul," Linda whispered, "I felt so bad, I tossed it around in my mind for a few days, I went back and forth a million times before I did it. I didn't want to leave any of you, but I was in such a dark place that I couldn't even help myself. I see that now. When Mom and Dad came to see me here—they were just so confused. And my friends... it was horrible." Paul heard her voice waver and assumed she had started to cry again. This made him cry more.

"But I'm different now, really, I am. I feel so much healthier. So much less guilty. These last 60 years I've been doing everything I could to make up for it. And I'm finally, finally starting to come to terms with it. Even if it doesn't seem like it." The decisiveness in her voice made the words sound more like a mantra than a sentence.

Paul peeked from under his forearm and looked at her. She rubbed her eyes and smiled sadly at him, a mix between satisfied and uncomfortable. He looked at her eyes and saw his eyes, and his mother's eyes, and his grandfather's eyes, and realized that he was capable of something like forgiveness.

Paul looked at his watch and then to Her, standing just out of his eyeline.

"I think," She shuffled paperwork, "I can spare you another 30 minutes."

After rubbing his eyes dry, Paul hoisted himself up.

"Paul," Linda whined, "say something. Anything."

Paul crossed and uncrossed his legs, trying to get comfortable, but unable to.

"Can we go back to the couch? I'm pretty sure I'm a lot older than you; this isn't a position I've been in for a long time."

Linda laughed and stood, offering a hand to Paul, helping him up. He sensed a metaphor but didn't want to let it take up space in his brain. He patted Linda on the shoulder amicably and walked back towards the room. Linda followed, She didn't.

Stepping into the room a second time, Paul noticed a clear difference in its original set up, namely that it looked like his parents' basement instead of the trendy living room he thought it was. The basement was recreated perfectly, from the record player console under the gallery wall of photos to the pillows with marijuana leaves his grandma had sewn, not realizing what the print looked like. The fireplace, the wiry carpet, the couches of a thousand different colored strings—all of it, perfect. Paul made a bee-line to the record player and right where it always was sat *Songs from the Big Chair* by Tears for Fears, the best album Paul ever found at a thrift store.

"The point of a record is to listen to the whole thing. Don't just skip to your favorites," he heard Linda say. Paul scoffed and caught a glimpse of his hands, which looked suspiciously younger. He turned abruptly to look at Linda, who put a hand over her mouth to suppress laughter.

"Oh yeah, you look younger. You look 15 again. Pimples and all."

Paul touched his face in horror, also full-on touching a glasses lens. He yanked off his glasses and furiously cleaned them on the hem of his shirt.

"I can't believe this," he muttered.

"I can. This is the last memory we have together that was normal. Remember?" She had made it over to the console and transitioned into leaning against it. Paul put his glasses back on and joined her.

"This is such a good album," Paul muttered, nodding his head in time.

"Yeah. It's a good thing mom was an alt kid growing up, or else we never would have had such a good collection to start with."

Paul felt a smile creep over his face. "Thanks for leaving me your personal record collection, by the way." Linda began to chuckle. "My kids loved playing the old vinyl. Some they appreciated more than others—they never really understood your Gowan obsession."

Linda put her hand on her face in embarrassment. "Oh, *god*. I remember. I loved him! Jenna and I went to see him in concert and I almost fainted." She zoned out for a moment, and Paul saw her smile fade and her eyes become sad again.

"Paul, I—"

"I don't think I'm ready to forgive you yet. I'm not sure—that's on me, though. Don't blame yourself. I have enough emotional intelligence to know that... it's not your fault I'm upset. But—" He was cut off by a knock on the door. Linda inhaled sharply.

"But. But I love you. You're my cool older sister. I want to talk to you. I want to move on. I think it'll hit me, you know, all at once." He looked down at his feet, ashamed and exhausted. "I just want to talk about something else. Is that okay? I'm sorry," he said.

He could hear a smile in Linda's voice when she said, "Sure, Paul. Okay," and put her hand on his shoulder.

"Well, you know all about my life," she said. "The 'we're watching over you from beyond' thing doesn't happen in the Temple, so I know nothing about your life. You said you had kids—and until a few minutes ago you were an old man." She wrapped her arm around his shoulder and rubbed her head against his. "Tell me about the last 60 years, while we still have time. Please."

Somehow it felt as though much longer than 15 minutes had passed between them. They had almost finished playing all their records when She came in, indicating it was time to go.

"Wait, how—how was *that* 15 minutes?" Paul said from the floor beside the console.

"It wasn't," She shrugged. "Something about diamonds and pressure and stuff." Paul and Linda both looked at Her, mouths open.

"Whatever. It worked. God's plan and all that."

"We've had enough time, Paul," Linda said, gently, interrupting whatever he was going to say. She started putting records away, carefully making sure that their inner and outer sleeves didn't have matching openings. "This was the last conversation I needed to have—you know, for the *process.*" Paul stood up and just looked at her, stony faced.

"You have stuff to see, though! Explore and whatnot— come to terms with your existence, man." Paul scoffed and thought that Linda was always such a hippy, and that she would say something like that.

"Before you go, let's take a picture though. I have a little mural in my room of photos. I have one of mom and dad and Jenna when she came—Ron, Sarah. All of the people I hurt when I—left." Paul could feel the knife that stabbed into her when she said that. Linda didn't look at Paul as she fished an old digital camera out of her jeans pocket that couldn't have been there the whole time. "I asked for one just for this purpose. Look at the photos I have!" Linda seemed elated to be showing Paul these photos—he saw his parents, and Ron, who was the first person to give him a cigarette, and Jenna, who was like a sister to Paul—and Sarah, gorgeous, excellent Sarah, the first girl he ever developed feelings for that proved to be extremely out of his league.

"Do we have a minute?" For the most part, She had stood silently, watching, but She was more than willing to take a photo on Linda's mediocre digital camera. She seemed happy, even. Linda wrapped her arms around Paul, who was shorter than her in his 15-year-old body, and She snapped several photos of the two of them smiling, hugging, and two or more of them making funny faces. Paul realized, then, that this was enough; that this was a happy ending to their relationship.

Linda kissed him on the forehead, "I love you, Paul."

"I love you, too, Linda," Paul whispered, his eyes closing and his body sinking.

As he opened his eyes, he realized Linda was gone and they were in a lobby. He knew it was a lobby because it was the lobby of his apartment building, where he had started his journey.

"Back at the beginning," She said lightly. Paul was trapped in his mind, running through his interaction with Linda over and over and regretting so much of what he said. She pulled him out by saying, "Should we go up?"

What would he find if he did? He had died in his easy chair, alone, in his sleep.

"No, I don't think we should."

She walked up to the front desk and rang the bell haphazardly. No one came to answer. "You don't want to see what's up there?" She asked, looking at Her fingernails.

Paul looked around and shook his head.

"Is there something you're scared of seeing?"

A chill went through Paul's body. "Something I'm scared of *not* seeing," he said with all the courage he could muster.

She nodded slowly, as if trying to comprehend what he was saying. She shrugged casually and they were instantly teleported into some sort of garden. She started to walk, and Paul followed apprehensively.

"Is this more comfortable for you?" She posited, looking over Her shoulder at him. Paul walked a little faster to catch up to Her and said that it was definitely better than being in his dingy lobby. She looked up at the sky and referred to a wrist watch he hadn't noticed before.

"Do you have any questions you want to ask while we have some time? Usually people ask stuff at this point."

Paul thought for a moment, thinking about what kind of questions he wanted answers to. He started with the easiest one he could think of: "So, Jesus? Real?"

She clasped Her hands behind Her back and nodded, "Yep. You can meet him if you want, but he's usually pretty busy doing other stuff."

"Mohammed?"

"Real."

"Abraham?"

"Real."

"Krishna?"

"Real," She exclaimed, laughing. "Everyone you're going to ask about is most definitely real. In some way or another." Paul nodded and then stopped abruptly, "Are we in the Garden of Eden?"

She laughed, and it reminded Paul of the first time he heard his wife laugh. He couldn't put his finger on it then, but after some contemplation, he understood. "Yes, we are. Pretty cool, huh?" She grabbed a fruit Paul couldn't recognize off of a tree, and before he could ask whether that was okay, She took a bite. "That was bullshit, you know. It was all a ploy."

She spoke again through bites of fruit. "What do you want for your last wish?"

Suddenly, Paul felt like he was falling again. Another commonly held belief shattered by reality. "I thought I got three wishes? I've only used one!"

He walked up to Her and stood abashedly by the fruit tree She had collapsed under. She laid with Her elbows propping up Her body and the pit of the strange fruit shuffling between Her fingers. Paul grunted as he gingerly put himself down under the tree beside Her.

"No one told you you got three. You assumed based on some corny film trope." She crushed the pit between Her fingers, turning it into dust that floated away. "We've found that two is usually enough."

Paul hadn't seen this coming; he was unsure of what a second wish—no, he thought, his last—could be. He had waited his whole life to see his sister again and ask her questions; now he had no idea what more he could possibly want. He was embarrassed at the fact that he hadn't thought this far.

"I'll give you a moment. Even though there was no reason for you to assume you had three wishes, I know this has thrown you for a loop." Another fruit appeared in Her hands—a pomegranate? —and She spoke, again. "By the way, you can't alter time."

Paul sat for a few moments before he came to the realization that She had been waiting for him to come to, making Her interjection understandable. He looked off into the distance and toyed with the words he wanted to say to make his wish into something coherent, because he had a feeling it worked that way.

"How vague can I get?" he asked, still not looking at Her.

She picked at Her fingernails and said, reassuringly, "Pretty vague. I'm pretty sure I can fill in the blanks."

"I wish to see what would have happened if—If I had done it differently," Paul said, definitively. She cracked Her knuckles and a large screen appeared, like they had set up a sheet and projector in a backyard somewhere.

"Not many people wish for this, you know, but when people do, they typically get flustered seeing it in their own mind. We've found that this helps with the *process*." Paul was now painfully aware of the word, and all of its implications.

What appeared on the screen was a younger Paul and his wife, Carrie. They were arguing while Carrie held a baby. There was no sound, but Paul knew this moment by heart because he had replayed it time and time again in his head for 35 years. Young Paul stormed out of the house while Carrie held the baby and cried. The scene followed Paul to the car. In the original timeline, if you will, Paul sat in his car for twenty minutes, and then drove to a woman's house. The affair would continue for 16 months, after which Carrie would promptly divorce Paul and take their children, the oldest of which was 12. The woman, Melissa, also broke things off with Paul upon finding out he was married. Paul would see his children often, as he and Carrie would begin to get along for their sake, but he pined after her, sleeping with many a Carrie look-alike for years, while she remarried and got her PhD. Paul resented her for her happiness because he was immature and selfish—he believed that he deserved forgiveness at the time. As he got older and wiser, and started going to therapy, he didn't.

He was about to speak when She said, "Keep watching. It *is* different."

Young Paul never even started the car, opting instead to slam the door closed and walk back into the house, where Carrie was. She was pretending to be asleep in their bed. He laid down next to her and whispered something inaudible, but what Paul guessed was "I'm sorry". He always wished he could go back and say that to her at that moment.

Carrie turned over and, with tears streaming down her face, kissed him hard. She mumbled something, Paul guessed, "It's okay", and they held each other until they fell asleep.

Paul began to sob, and the projection paused. "Does it end the way I think it does?" he said through chaotic tears.

"Let's watch the whole thing," She said, and the life-movie kept playing.

At first the scenes were happy; Paul saw his kids grow up with Carrie by his side instead of alone, as he had been. The accomplishments were the same—his oldest daughter was still a doctor, his second daughter was still a soldier, and his two youngest sons were still in college, but Carrie was there with him. He clapped for her when she walked across the stage at her own graduation ceremony, accepting her Doctorate in Philosophy. He noticed her getting sadder and sadder. Then he noticed the two of them fighting more and more. Eventually the same scene happened where Paul stormed out and drove somewhere, except this time he and Carrie were older, and his kids were moved out. Carrie didn't cry this time, and Paul didn't drive to a woman's house; he simply drove to a hotel.

The next few scenes felt like they were immediately after each other, but still millions of years apart. There were separation papers, protestations from one of the children (the youngest of the two youngest sons) while the others were ambivalent, taking no sides. Then the divorce papers, the settlement, and, eventually, Paul alone in his apartment. The apartment looked brighter, somehow, than he remembered it, but he was still an old man with a lonely job and a lonely house. He began to cry because everything ended up the same, and he realized the futility of fighting the unstoppable tide of destiny.

She patted his shoulder gingerly while he cried.

He turned to Her angrily, "I thought humans had free will? How did it end up the same?"

She sighed and looked at him sadly. "I don't know. I honestly don't have all the answers. I'm just as upset about it as you are."

Paul ran through everything that had happened and asked himself question after question. How could he have done anything differently? Could he have gone to therapy with Carrie? How did it end up the same?

After a millennium, She spoke again. "There's some comfort in this, though."

Paul couldn't see it and told her so.

"It means you probably did everything you could, you know?"

In that moment, all the questions he was asking himself culminated in one answer: No. Even if it didn't make grammatical sense, even if he didn't understand how, the answer to all his questions was just no. Maybe he *had* done everything he could have; if their separation was inevitable, then he should find peace in the fact that even his best couldn't stop what was meant for him. Maybe everything was actually just fine the way it had been. Maybe free will was one thing, but maybe destiny was another, stronger, more primal thing. Inescapable no matter what.

And in that moment, Paul was gone, and suddenly a baby named Charles in a small town in Quebec had a soul.

Pastiche

She was the kind of woman you just don't mess with. She really was, though it does seem cliché to start a story like that. Most of the time when I would see her, she was standing on the balcony of her room smoking what I later learned were Natives, cigarettes made or bought on reserves and known for being stronger than normal cigarettes and sometimes having feathers in them. She was staying in the room on the top floor of the bed and breakfast my parents owned and I had worked at every summer since I was 15; it used to be the family cottage. I went to university for four years at NYU and majored in Philosophy. Because my two older brothers are physicians and my older sister is a surgeon, being the youngest, I got to sort of 'follow my dreams', as it were. Someone needed to work at the B&B and, because my parents were in their 60s by the time I finished university, and my siblings weren't really able to 'leave their lives' and 'completely relocate' to the sleepy town of Bala, Ontario, Canada, that someone was me. One of my brothers works in Bracebridge, a town not far away, but far enough that he doesn't have to help with the family business unless something goes wrong. My other two siblings are both in Michigan, one in Detroit and one in Lansing. I was the only one who could help them out, and I didn't mind even though I did make a fuss about it. I just didn't want my 'successful' siblings telling me what to do.

I had actually met this woman, who called herself Tara (I still believe it is a fake name), when I was 24, a couple years into my time working the B&B. Up until then there were some interesting people. One couple asked if they could have a room with an attached bathroom because they were into weird sex stuff—like, I mean, weird is probably a rude way to put it, but to me it was just strange. One of the maids we employed said that she caught the woman with her head literally in the toilet and the man flushing it—like he was giving her a swirly. The two were also completely naked. But that maid is only 17 and prone to telling stories which might not be true. I can't really fathom how someone could enjoy this kind of behavior from a sexual standpoint but, as a semi-virgin, I suppose my opinion doesn't really count. Either way, I'm pretty sure the maid, Sandra, was lying or at least exaggerating. Sandra was alright, though. We made out a few times but never went any farther than that because, of course, she was under age and her parents both had guns. We always made quite a bit of money during the year—even in winter—and there were always people who were interesting, but not *interesting*. Tara was the most *interesting* person I'd met at the B&B, and I'm pretty sure I'll never meet anyone like her again.

I was 24 at the time and bored out of my mind. I had a degree in Philosophy, so I spent most of my time listening to old people try to tell me why gay marriage was an abomination and Socratic Method-ing the shit out of them. I couldn't stand ignorance like that. When I got time, which was surprisingly not often, I would continue a mural I had begun earlier that summer. I wasn't doing anything I had thought of; I was recreating a painting by a forger who'd made a painting in the style of Raoul Dufy that matched our décor. Our B&B appeared effortlessly rustic, but my mother had hired a professional interior decorator to intentionally design it that way. The whole property was meant to feel like a home hidden within a forest, with wrought iron balconies and a substantial amount of grey brick. I plastered over one portion of the wall so I could paint more easily and began painting the Dufy forgery, titled *The Letter (in the style of Raoul Dufy)*. There's a woman sitting on a bench in the painting, so I was going to make a bench to put in the spot where she would be to make it a whole piece, you know? Just to make the backyard a little more *interesting*. I was playing Lera Lynn on a small iPod dock and, since it was a slow week, I could play it loudly without disturbing many people. I was sitting there, almost cheerily painting with a cigarette in my mouth, when Tara came up behind me so silently she startled me when she spoke.

"Dufy is a painter I really enjoy, too." She spoke deliberately, like I do when I'm trying too consciously not to be condescending.

"Jesus Christ, hi. You are, like, exceptionally silent," I said stupidly.

"Yeah." She laughed and threw her head back. I squinted in a way that I believed was imperceptible. This felt too much like a film, too much déjà vu—this is how people meet in stories, not real life; a meet-cute for the ages. "I heard Lera Lynn and came out to size up the person at this place with impeccable taste. Who would've thought it was you!" We didn't even know each other, and she was making fun of me. I could feel myself falling in love.

"She's fantastic, isn't she? The good thing about living up here is that if you listen to music that's even vaguely country, you're allowed to play it pretty loudly." I paused and stretched a little, feeling things crack and creak. "I hope I didn't disturb you, though."

"Not at all. I was going to go for a walk anyway. The grounds here are fantastic. Whoever works them does a spectacular job. And I'm not even being hyperbolic—I really get the feeling that I'm in a small castle." I stood up as she was speaking, not wanting to be rude to this stunning creature. She had turned to look at the garden, and probably sensing I had stood up, she turned back to face me. I looked into her eyes and I felt like I saw her completely. You ever get that feeling? As though you've been afforded a special opportunity to actually see into someone's soul? People say that, looking into one's eyes, you can see the inner workings of one's mind, but I rarely get that feeling. People are easy to manipulate, easy to understand, but rarely willing to be vulnerable. With Tara, though, I felt like I saw everything— but by accident. She instantly, though subtly, blocked off whatever I saw. But it was too late. I had seen the hurt deep inside of her and the anger closer to the surface.

I decided to stay away from any deep conversation and steered towards the regular kind, slightly disappointed. "It's a combo of our paid groundskeepers and my control-freak mother. She has a green thumb, as they say. She does most of the flowers, or delegates their planting, whereas the gardeners do the tough, subtle stuff." I pointed to the ivy going up the wall beside my painting, "The gardeners do stuff like this," I then pointed to the hibiscus bushes at the base of the wall, "and my mother does stuff like that."

I suppose Tara loosened up a little and decided to flirt when she smiled and said, "Well, what do you do around here? Besides paint exterior walls beautifully?" I couldn't help but smile because she *was* adorable, but I could tell she was being completely two-dimensional, which I wasn't enjoying, to be honest, despite her beauty.

"Me? Painting exterior walls is a clever way to put it, if you include the part where I watch the paint dry. I'm the designated brooder, as my mom calls me. I sit behind the front desk and brood, or I talk to guests and brood. I even paint and brood sometimes." I began to pack up my supplies, intending to do something—like clean, because this was still my place of work despite it being owned by my parents—because the conversation between Tara and I was getting tedious. I felt like I was being used, because she was beautiful and I was me, and that's just what pretty people do.

"No, no, don't stop on my account. I really am going to go for a walk. I'll be seeing you!" She saluted me as she made her way into the garden and I waved goodbye. I frowned to myself, hoping I hadn't missed an opportunity, but opting for apathy instead of regret.

I would often fall asleep at the front desk because it was the only place I could get Wi-Fi and I was trying to learn German online. Because someone had to be at the desk or within earshot of the phone at all times, I had a little sleeping mat on the floor under the desk and would sometimes fall onto it and sleep. I used my own computer to run the books, since I lived there, and I would sometimes write or online shop, too. I wasn't constantly brooding. I did enjoy my job to some degree, I just didn't enjoy the people, who definitely could be horrid. Normally they were just average and boring and that was sort of worse.

That previous paragraph puts the next part of the story into context, because why would I be answering the desk phone in the middle of the night if I wasn't near it somehow? The reason I answered the phone was because someone was calling, of course, and that someone was Tara.

"Front desk," I said, groggy because I had just been dead asleep on the floor.

"Hey. It's Tara, in the top floor room?" She sounded on edge, like someone holding a gun to someone's head, unsure of what to do next. I pushed away the thought.

"Yep, Tara, hey. What can I do for you?" I rubbed my eyes and slapped my face a little to sound less gross.

"Well, it says here that I can call the front desk and ask for anything, and even though it seems like an exaggeration, I'm wondering if I could ask a favor? You seem like a pretty cool person and you can probably help me with something." I was flattered and tired, so I had very mixed feelings about her proposition.

"It's definitely just an exaggeration, but I'll see if I can help. What can I do for you?" I had been on the floor when I answered but had since moved up into the desk chair. I checked my computer to see what tabs I had open and began closing and bookmarking unimportant and important ones, half listening. Usually, when people called in the middle of the night it was so they could get condoms or the number for a pizza place that was open late.

"Well, uh," she paused. "Just... could you drive me somewhere? You drive, right?" She was shuffling in the background.

"Yeah, I do," I said, as I fished around the desk drawers for the keys to the old Toyota I sometimes drove. I usually took my bike if I had to go anywhere. I knew she had driven to the B&B but her having access to her own vehicle didn't even dawn on me. It was as though we were in a movie, and only I could help. It was also a lot more *interesting* to go with her than to remind her she didn't need me to drive her anywhere. "Meet me in the front. But we should be quick—I have to 'monitor the desk', you know?" I legitimately did air quotes, although no one was there. Force of habit, I suppose.

We met on the porch, and when she came downstairs, she had a baseball bat. Did she pack it, or did she buy it somewhere in town? I wondered but didn't ask. She was wearing all black, and I realized I was, too. I guess that was appropriate, because I was sure we were about to do some fucked up shit.

"Alright, let's go," she said, quite seriously. She was wearing a hat I later learned was a balaclava. She started walking and, comically, turned back to me and said, "Wait, where's your car, even?" I pointed in the opposite direction, and we walked towards the car, about fifty paces from the house.

At some point, I asked, "Where are we going?"

She looked over to me and said, quite seriously, "To fuck shit up."

I couldn't help but laugh, and she laughed too, briefly, before saying, "No seriously, we're going to fuck shit up. Drive out of here, I'll direct you."

We drove, making lefts, and rights, and U-turns when she wouldn't tell me to turn soon enough. We eventually made it to a cottage that was semi-remote, and my Toyota was feeling it. The cottage itself was average; two stories, possibly a basement, there seemed to be the hint of a boathouse somewhere behind it. I was unimpressed, which I felt guilty for, but then immediately stopped caring. I looked to my right and Tara had pulled the balaclava over her face and turned to me.

"You may be wondering what we're doing here," she said, looking me right in the eyes.

"Not really. You said we were doing some fucked up shit, so, that's what I'm going with." I shrugged. There were three reasons I wasn't worried about getting in a lot of trouble, and three reasons were all I needed.

One: This cottage was secluded, and no one would be able to get here for at least 30 minutes, which would give us either enough time to hide somewhere or drive back to the main road. There was another cottage about 15 minutes down the road, it seemed (the road didn't end at this cottage so I assumed it wasn't the last one), so we could always say we came from there.

Two: my family knew literally every cop in this town. They would come with their significant others to our B&B for their cop dinner or whatever. I knew they would recognize me, and I was not worried that they would prosecute me if we did anything minor.

Three: We probably weren't going to do anything that fucked up, right? I mean, I was voting against murder.

Those were my reasons, and I stuck to them. At this point, you may find me slightly sociopathic, but I encourage you to keep reading because I am not the fucked up one in this story, I assure you.

The cottage seemed deserted, even though there was a car in the modest driveway. I got the feeling no one was up there that weekend, but that it was a frequently-used cottage. There was a substantial amount of foliage around, but it was kept clean, the way you would make a niece or nephew, or grandkid, keep it clean whenever they came up.

Tara snickered while I observed, and said, "You got it, dude. Don't worry, it's nothing that should be too troublesome. This cottage doesn't have cameras, as you may be able to tell." She got out of the car and grabbed her baseball bat. She looked foxy, like a comic book character or something, standing there with the baseball bat over her shoulder and her one arm akimbo. Then, everything got a little crazy.

She walked up to the car and bashed the driver's side window in. The alarm started to go off, but Tara opened the door and somehow shut off the alarm. She proceeded to ransack the middle compartment/arm rest, and I suppose found whatever she had wanted to find, because she put something in her pocket. She got out of the car and started hitting its flank with her bat, denting it. She walked to the back of the car and smashed the lights, then climbed on top of the trunk and started jumping on the hood, which was no small feat considering the stilettos she was wearing. She held the top of the bat with two hands and used the hilt to continue denting the hood. It was at that moment I snapped out of my mini-coma and got out of my car, whisper-screaming, 'What the fuck, Tara,' about 30 times until I reached her.

She jumped off the car on the passenger side and kicked the window in, shattering it, just like my expectations of the 'fucked up shit' we were going to do—good one, eh?

"What did you think we were going to do?" she said, breathing hard and doubled over, as if she had read my mind.

"Um, usually 'fucked up shit' around here means, like, baseball with mailboxes, not fucking destroying someone's car!" I was infuriated, and afraid, because I really didn't think my connections could get me out of this.

"Listen, I'll explain some other time. Right now, we should go—I've done my damage." She stood up and walked towards my car in a way that made me feel as though she was feeling really good about herself while I was losing my shit. I stood, my mouth agape, before she said, "Holy fuck, we have to get out of here—let's go!" in an exasperated tone.

"Don't get fucking exasperated, goddamnit!" I sputtered trying to find something cool to say and coming out with that. I remember thinking, 'I have a philosophy degree and *that's* the best I can do?'.

I got into the car and floored it back to the B&B. She was quiet on the ride back, and I was too paranoid to start a conversation. We made it back without anything happening, but it was still tense, at least for me. Tara seemed fine.

We sat in the car, saying nothing. She pulled a cigarette out of nowhere and began smoking, and I was too shocked to stop her from smoking in my relatively pristine car. I pulled my emergency joint out of the glove compartment and was surprised that it wasn't rancid. I put my hand out, and, reading my mind, Tara put her lighter in it. I lit up, not caring anymore, wanting to spend my last moments of freedom baked.

She spoke in an almost whisper, but I heard it. She said, "A man goes up a tree, people throw rocks at the man, the man comes down from the tree, having changed," and got out of the car. I was too ambivalent towards the woman who was going to get me thrown in a totally un-sexy jail for some sort of, what I assumed to be, crime of passion.

I sat in the car, finished my jay, and hobbled to the front desk to sleep, noticing that the whole world seemed like something I only half knew—something familiar and foreign—as though I had suddenly emerged from the Cave in Plato's *The Republic*. It could have been the semi-rancid weed, but I think it was just me.

The next day she was obviously gone. I mean, as if this story wasn't filled with enough clichés already. I was the first one in her room after she left—the coffee maker was still on. I had gone up there to talk to her, but all I found was a note, because of course.

"Hey gorgeous,

Thanks for all your help. You don't know how much it meant to me. The credit card I gave you was fake, but the money on the dresser is real—it's your rate plus a little extra for you—just you, and your paintings. You probably have a lot of questions, but I can only answer one, so choose wisely.

I hope your question was, "What could the owner of that car possibly done?" The short story? He grabbed my ass in a bar. The long story? One day I'll tell you the whole thing. I'll be back in a while, so try not to quit the B&B life for a while—or forever. Maybe I'll never come back, but I can't make this note so long that you won't be able to burn it easily. I can't thank you enough, though, again. One day I hope to tell you the whole story, but it's filled with clichés and it's probably not justification enough for what I did to his car—at least, that's what some people will undoubtedly tell me.

Parting is such sweet sorrow, etc etc. I left you clues around the B&B as to what my phone number is. If you ever find out what it is, call me. I'll buy you coffee, if you drink coffee. I realize now that I put a lot of faith in you, and you a lot in me. Hopefully this experience taught you how to trust again, my friend.

Love,
You know"

And that was literally all she wrote. The next six months I searched frantically for the numbers and found six of them. Then I sort of gave up, like when you half-heartedly take a picture of a sunset because you know it looks beautiful, but you just don't feel in awe of it. The difference is, I still felt in awe of Tara—but it was a more *aware* kind of awe, you know? Maybe she never actually wanted me to find her number.

It's been about five years, and no word. I'm not mad, really. I've enjoyed the B&B. I finished my painting within those first six months, and now we're doing some remodeling in the kitchens as per the chef's request. My dad passed away two years ago, and my siblings promised to 'help out more' and 'be there more', but I've seen them less than when he was alive. Everyone handles grief differently, I guess. I still paint, and sometimes I blog, but mostly I just exist in a state of insecurity, waiting for Tara to come back and feeling like an idiot because of it.

Anyway. Tara, if you're reading this—I *do* drink coffee.

Discussion Question: What gender is the narrator?

If You Can't Beat 'Em

Marla loved her job.

Though some days she dreaded the commute or didn't go to bed early enough the night before, once she got into work, all her hatred for her nine to five melted away. She enjoyed the routine of it all, her coworkers, and best of all—she felt as though she was *actually* making a difference.

Marla's day started with a calendar check. Often her appointments were scheduled between one and three on Mondays and Tuesdays, while Wednesday through Friday she did her research. Marla enjoyed spending hours creating a sim. She usually worked from a state-sanctioned template, but she could get creative—in fact, some said that was what made her so good at her job.

Marla had the most seniority in her department through a series of premature departures. Many people couldn't do what came so easily to her, and while it was annoying to try to hire, train, and then shuffle her schedule to take over the appointments that were dropped because of a resignation, Marla did understand that this was an especially difficult job for some people. She petitioned to have a mandatory personality test, psych eval, and level 7A clearance, dumbfounded that somehow these necessities hadn't been mandatory but rather *implied* (and often not *actually* followed by her 'superiors'), and though for a while there were a few employees on her floor, eventually they got too close to a case or it hit them too hard and they would quit. Sad but true, she would say to her friends in other departments. Not everyone can hack it. Sometimes they'd say they weren't sure how *she* hacked it all these years, none of them knowing exactly what she did because they lacked the clearance but knowing that if they needed authorization to know what she did, it was probably a scary and/or difficult job.

Unfortunately, today was what Marla hoped would be the beginning of the end—she had spent 10 years doing a job that she enjoyed. It was time for her to transition into something different, something not so difficult. She dreamed about opening a pub in Hawaii or Cuba, somewhere warm. Marla had nothing tying her to this godforsaken city anymore and needed a change of pace. She thought about leaving often, and today she had finally taken at least a baby step in the right direction.

Marla walked into work on this particular morning somewhat disheveled. This case was giving her a lot of trouble. The perp's lawyer kept pushing his punishment—or rehabilitation, as she was contractually obligated to call it—for arbitrary reasons. First it was because Marla's sim was too graphic (an impossible claim, given that it was only as graphic as the perp's own fucking actions, Marla told her boss at the time), then it was because the lawyer had a court date and couldn't make it to the session and she wanted to be there to see the goings on, as she had never been to see a sim before (and in Marla's opinion, never seemed to care), and then on the third attempt at pushing the date Marla filed an official complaint against the lawyer for obstruction and the date was set. She sat down at her desk and looked through the sim one last time, uncomfortable and proud. Marla made her way out of her office and was stopped by Greg, her superior.

"Morning, Marl! How's it going?" Greg was so unreasonably chipper Marla almost didn't notice the human beside him; a lady in her twenties, the strong but silent type with a kind face. Marla refrained from audibly sighing, realizing exactly where this was going.

"Morning, Gregory. I'm not here to fuck spiders." A favourite phrase of Marla's that was often said around Greg who always seemed to waste her time. She was not a fan of Greg, and he was not a fan of her, but they had a rapport.

"Marla, this is Terry. Terry, this is Marla. Marla will be training you today on sims. I believe she has a particularly interesting case today, right Marl?" He had his hand on Terry's shoulder in such a way that indicated to Marla either he was interested in her, knew her personally, or wanted to use her as a human shield to deflect Marla's eye-daggers. Marla wasn't a mean person—she just didn't like Greg.

Marla put her hand out to Terry and gave her a "nice to meet you" while sizing her up. Marla's first impression of Terry was fairly positive, mostly because in Terry she saw a possible escape, as if the universe was trying to send her a sign. Terry was taller than Marla and thinner, but she had a strong handshake which, to her, indicated confidence despite a plain face and a skin color that still wasn't trendy. Marla immediately empathized, being of a particularly unpopular type herself. Marla liked Terry immediately.

"Now, today is going to be a *day* so if there's nothing else, Greg, I'd like to get started."

"Of course. You two gals have fun!" Greg said, walking away. Marla and Terry both rolled their eyes.

"You see how he said that as he was walking away? It's so that he could avoid me calling him out. Gross." Marla began to walk towards her original destination, the sim lab. Terry followed.

"Do you think he knows he sucks, or...?" Terry trailed off.

Marla scoffed, "Absolutely not. He has a picture of himself in his office. And not, like, him and his family. Just him. It's gross."

"Is *that* what that picture is on his desk!" Terry exclaimed. "What an oddball."

"Anyway, I'd hate to give that *dweeb* any more of my brain time or oxygen. Right now, we're walking to the sim lab. I'll give you the full tour later. Right now, this appointment has been pushed off so many times that I just want to get it the *fuck* over with." Marla stopped short and looked at Terry intensely. "They told you what I do here, right?"

Terry mumbled that she had an idea, but no one would come right out and say it, but she did have the clearance and passed the psych test. Marla frowned.

"Okay," she sighed. What could she do at this point? If Marla had had more time, she would have run Terry through the whole thing, told her the slightly false version of how this department got its start, and eased her into it. She would've picked a more cut and dry case, or at least an easier one for Terry's first. What could Marla do but embrace the fact that this was the hand they had been dealt and that, unfortunately, today she had to rip off the band aid. Maybe it would make Terry a more suitable candidate or—Marla hesitated to think—a suitable replacement.

"I think we had better just dive in headfirst. I *will* give you some warning, though—it's not an easy job and it sure as hell isn't a nice one, but it is, in some ways, vindicating." Marla kept walking and Terry kept following.

"Today we're working with a perp that has a pretty sneaky lawyer. I don't really like her very much. She kept pushing back the appointment on account of dumb shit and I just have no interest in communicating with her. Your job today will be to keep her off my back as well as learning the ropes. And thank you in advance for doing what you can to keep this—" Marla saw the lawyer, Sandra, waiting in front of the sim lab door and said under her breath, "Speak of the fucking devil."

Sandra was a stern-looking woman but also a rich-looking one. She had spent a lot of years defending criminals, taking their money, and getting work done on her face. Marla had known Sandra for a long time and knew what she was like in and out of court. Sandra had a smarmy smile that reminded Marla of a crocodile. Sandra was smiling when Marla and Terry walked up to the door of the lab.

"Marla! Great to finally see you. I can't believe how long this case's taken. Crazy, huh? Glad you finally got that sim all fixed up." Marla felt her eye twitch, but said nothing, only grunting in reply. Terry was a little more forthcoming, holding her hand out for Sandra to shake. Sandra, of course, refrained.

"New employee? How nice! Finally—you won't be so lonely on your floor. And it's been *ages* since you had any help. You must be looking forward to taking a load off, huh?" Sandra did the thing where she nudged Marla in the side in a friendly way. Marla stopped herself from yelling, 'don't fucking touch me', miraculously, and finished unlocking the door to the lab. Sandra and Terry followed.

The crim was already strapped in to the repurposed dentist chair, equipped with a ventilation mask that made it impossible to speak. Awake but immobilized, the man was looking around lazily, with seemingly no cares to perturb him. Marla especially hated crims like this, without remorse or empathy. Marla ignored her discomfort and proceeded with her job, reminding herself that she wasn't doing it for herself, but for his many victims. She was just happy he couldn't talk.

Sandra seemed agitated and let Marla know immediately. "This is positively inhumane!" Sandra cried, walking over to her client. "This is preposterous. How can you treat a human like this?" Sandra began to take out her phone, but Terry stepped in.

"You, presumably, signed a waiver when you decided you wanted to participate in the rehabilitation which states that you can't have your phone on you, *so* I'll actually have to confiscate it now."

"Absolutely not. I need this for my *job*, which, you know, doesn't involve *torturing* people." Marla scoffed, and Sandra shot her a look.

"Fine," Terry said, walking towards the intercom system by the door. "Then you'll have to be ejected from the room and maybe even the building. You signed the necessary paperwork—hello, I need security in here ASAP—and ultimately you being here is not necessary but, rather, a privilege offered to the legal representation of the client."

A friendly but frightening security guard named Marcus walked through the door and looked at Marla. "Everything okay, Marla?"

Marla was overjoyed. She smiled disgustingly at Sandra, who looked annoyed but slightly scared. "Well, firstly, Sandra here still has her phone on her, and it has definitely been compromised."

Marcus went to Sandra and held out his hand and said gently, "I'll have to take your phone, ma'am. We can't have phones in this area of the building due to confi—"

Sandra threw her hands in the air and they landed automatically on her hips. With her arms akimbo she reminded Marla of a flightless bird. "Absolutely you can*not* have my phone. I'll just leave. But, Marla," Sandra turned to Marla, "you'll have to answer for this torture one day."

Marla laughed out loud, obnoxiously. "*I'll* have to answer for my torture? You've *got* to be kidding me, Sandra." Marla walked over to her, like a snake crawls to its prey, years of torment, anguish, anger, and strife boiling to the surface, and said menacingly. "You'll have to answer for what you did to *me* one day, Sandra. Maybe not today or tomorrow, but one day, you'll wake up and you'll have *nothing*. Just like me. *Nothing*."

Marla skulked back to her station, waived her hand in the air telling Sandra to leave. Marla didn't look up, only tightened the straps of the crim on the slab. Sandra walked out with her nose in the air and a sour look on her face.

Marla saw Terry and Marcus look at each other. Marcus shrugged and patted Marla on the shoulder as he walked out. Terry awkwardly stood by the door until Marla said, "Can you help me over here for a sec?" Pointing to several tools, a small vial, and her laptop. "It's a little gruesome, actually, so I hope you have a strong stomach."

Terry pulled a roll-y-chair over to Marla and the dentist chair set up. Marla could sense she was enthusiastic, but thought that it was, perhaps, a little premature.

"Alright, so, we've been tinkering with the way to do this for about ten years now. We used to create an implant and put it in the crim's head and then attach what was basically a glorified USB cable between the computer and the crim."

"Like the thing Neo had in *the Matrix*?"

"Exactly. Then the third Technological Revolution happened, and we were able to actually get a fucking tech guy in here as well as a biochemist and neurosurgeon and we worked on a new method. Much cleaner, faster, and, some people might even say fortunately-slash-unfortunately, more humane. See that vial over there?"

Terry grabbed the small vial of pinkish liquid and handed it to Marla. "This is actually twelve million nanos. They're biodegradable and Bluetooth operated. Pass me the syringe?"

Terry passed Marla the syringe. "Oh, shit, we should put on some gloves. It's not super important right now but we don't want to forget. I always forget the fucking gloves until it's too late and I have to start over." Terry passed Marla a pair of lightly powdered gloves, which Marla hated. "Okay, we got our gloves," Marla inserted the syringe into the tube and withdrew almost all 12 million nanos.

"Alright, so, now we inject the nanos into the jugular," Marla stepped over to the crim, who presumably was hearing this. She found his vein and gently punctured it, pushing the plunger down and forcing the nanos into his bloodstream. The crim immediately began to writhe in pain. If he hadn't been strapped down the needle would've gone flying. His mouth opened wide as if to scream but there was only air. His eyes teared up from being unable to blink and his hands opened and closed in pain and anger.

Terry flinched and opened her eyes wide. "This is completely normal. It seems to be quite painful. I wouldn't know, but that's just what I've noticed," Marla said. She could tell Terry wasn't sure if she was being sarcastic.

"So now we give it about 20 minutes. Usually I step out and grab a coffee. Would you like to go for a walk?" Marla began to collect her phone and wallet, opting to leave everything else in the highly surveillanced room.

Terry's eyes seemed to search for something on the ground, and she let out a brief, 'coffee sounds good'. Marla nodded and walked towards the door, holding it open for Terry while the crim continued to silently scream and shake as though he were going through withdrawals.

Marla and Terry had to walk for four minutes to the elevator, take it down 16 flights, and then walk across the street to get to the nearest coffee shop. Marla had timed this, and it took about 17 minutes there and back, give or take how many people were getting into the elevator or grabbing coffee. Very few words were exchanged from door to door. Marla let Terry process, but because of her frequent exposure to the situation couldn't really empathize with how disturbing it was. In fact, for Sandra to call it torture wasn't exactly far off, but Marla didn't really see it that way. She would sometimes think about a short story she read in school about a society that was perfect in every way, but secretly kept a person in destitution. She had tried to look for the story but had a hard time wanting to find it.

When they made it back to the office, Marla was expecting Terry to bow out, maybe finish the day but not necessarily in the sim lab. Marla paused outside the door, ready to send Terry to the break room or something, but Terry opened the door to the lab and stepped in. Marla followed her in, grateful that she hadn't lost another recruit. The door auto-locked behind them.

"So, what do the nanos *do* exactly?" Terry queried, donning a new pair of gloves.

"Well, they're embedded with this crazy fungus that brainwashes ants into basically killing themselves. *Cordyceps unilateralis*. It's actually kind of gross, but it helps soften the brain, so to speak, acting as an anesthetic and adds a biological element, at the government's *behest*. Either way, the brain is pretty much completely under our control, so we don't really need to worry about our guys getting attacked or anything." Marla sighed and stretched in her chair. "Then, the nanos attach to the visual cortex, amygdala, and hippocampus. Sorry, is this jargon boring you?" Marla noticed Terry yawn and chuckled a bit.

"No, no. I just never had a thing for science. But I think I kind of get it. It's like you create a dream in their brain and control it like *Inception*." Terry situated herself behind the crim but close to Marla, with Marla taking her usual position in front of a computer adjacent to the sim-chair. "But wouldn't that just mean manipulating the amygdala and visual cortex? What's the use in hijacking the hippocampus?"

"Not into science, huh?" Marla looked up at Terry, and matter-of-factly stated by far the most fucked up part of the program. "We manipulate the hippocampus to make the crim believe the dream is real. The nanos, besides helping me latch into the crim's brain and operate it, take the neurons created when we put the crim through this sim and implant them in the hippocampus. Or at least that's what seems to happen and what all the science people tell me happens." Marla looked away from Terry as she explained how the nanos left the crim's system, a decidedly unpleasant experience for everyone, including the two of them.

Terry nodded slowly, taking it better than Marla expected. "And the fungus?"

"The nanos kill as much as they can, and just as a precaution they emit a sort of antidote to kill whatever remains. It's not *really* murderous to humans, it'll just make the crim really sick. Like, puke-y. The antidote was added after many complaints from corrections cleaning staff."

Marla mumbled an explanation of what she began doing, which was uploading the sim into the computer program so she could control it. Her least favorite part of her job was approaching, and that was the moment when Greg would inevitably stop by just to say he did. Marla wished he would just forgo the formality and leave her alone, but he never failed to show up. She expected he would take special pains to do so today, given it was Terry's first day.

Greg knocked as he attempted to open the locked door, and Marla, while rolling her eyes, asked Terry if she could open the door and let him in. Marla heard the door open but didn't look up to greet Greg in any way. He made his presence known, and Marla was forced to acknowledge him when he directly addressed her.

"You're not strapping Terry in?" Marla looked up at Greg, flabbergasted.

"Greg, I'm not putting her into this sim. It's her first day. I'm going to project it like I would for a vic who wanted to participate." Marla tried to sound reasonable but could tell she was probably coming off as condescending.

"She needs to learn Marla; I don't think we should pull punches—"

"Greg, I don't want to do this with you today," Marla massaged the bridge of her nose and looked up at the ceiling. "Have you ever been strapped into a sim, Greg?"

"Yes!" he exclaimed.

"Yes, and Greg how *long* were you strapped into the sim for before you had to bow out—which is totally okay, by the way—like, five minutes? It's not shameful to back out of a sim, but she should just see what they're like before we put her through the paces." Greg paused and Marla wondered how much of a fight he was willing to put up. She knew she was right to take it slow, given how Terry reacted to the crim being strapped in. Marla had seen Terry's reaction, not Greg.

"If I could interject," Terry stepped in between Greg and Marla. "I would prefer to not be *strapped in* or anything today—"

"Strapped in just means you can control the sim, you obviously wouldn't be strapped in the same way the crim is, by the way. It's still a really vivid and almost tangible experience, and I wouldn't expect you to be ready on your first day. That's how you lose people, Greg." Marla scoffed pointedly.

"Either way, I'd rather just get to know the ins and outs today if that's okay, Greg."

Marla looked at him harshly, daring him to force Terry to do something. Marla was composing the email to HR in her head when Greg shrugged and mumbled something about not being able to force anyone into doing anything. There was subsequently a brief exchange between Greg and Marla wherein Greg said he would be back later, and Marla grunted. Terry stood meekly on Marla's left, seeming like she wanted to say something.

"What is it?"

"He just seemed a little peeved and I don't want you to get in shit or anything."

"No, don't worry about that." Marla looked up from her paperwork and massaged her nose. "It's good you spoke up. It validated what I was saying—and Greg *knew* that strapping you in would be a poor choice today, he just wanted to provide a contrary opinion."

Marla fired up the sim on the screen and Terry turned to face it, crossing and uncrossing her legs in what Marla assumed was an attempt to get comfortable. The sim looked like a first-person shooter video game on pause—if the first-person shooter started out in a pretty mundane coffee shop type setting. Marla strapped herself in, meaning she put on a pair of glasses whereby she could see the sim in more detail and calibrated her controls. "State of the art," she said, swiping her fingers in the air, thus starting the sim.

The sims were never particularly long. Often they were only about 20 minutes in real time with about a half hour of preamble and set up. The crim did experience the sim differently though, and when Marla was strapped in so did she. She could go in and out of seeing it from the crim's perspective, but often it made sense to spend most of her time under in case the crim broke away from the sim. This sim started in a coffee shop.

The crim, let's call him Val, was sitting in a shop and reading. A warm feeling of contentment permeated throughout his being upon noticing that a beautiful man was looking at him and seemed interested. The same man, let's call him Grady, approached Val and the two began to talk about books, and art.

"This book," Val says, "is one of my favorites. I read it as a child, and I pick it back up every now and again." Marla had done a lot of research into Val's likes and dislikes. Those details were what made the actual simulated crime so much more chilling. Marla knew that the book in question

was *Homo Deus* by Yuval Noah Harari, and that Val liked
it because of its subject matter, even if he was completely
misreading it for his own confirmation bias.

"I loved that book. I read it a while ago," Grady said,
perking up. "There's a great bookshop around here—if you
have some time today, we should go!"

Val showed some trepidation, but he ultimately trusted
Grady for reasons he couldn't explain. Marla checked Val's
brain signals and saw that all the emotions he was feeling
were in line with what he was supposed to be feeling at this
point. Sometimes crims would get suspicious at this point
and break out a little, doubt peeking through at the beginning
of a sim. Val was playing right into Marla's hands.

"But we've only just met!"

"Be adventurous! It's just up the street. You'll love it, it's
got every book you can think of." The two left the coffee shop
and walked up the street to the bookshop.

Val hadn't gotten to read a lot of books growing up because
his family lived in abject poverty. *Homo Deus* was among his
father's educational books, and Val was only able to read it
when his father was asleep. Val loved books, though, and
often he would take several from the apartments of women
he abducted. Marla had studied him intently and noticed
that in his testimonies, he always seemed to describe the
women he took in romantic but ultimately hateful ways—she
reasoned that he sounded like a jilted lover. She had also
noticed that his file was filled with petty assault cases on gay
men and extrapolated that perhaps there were some latent
homosexual feelings in the man that were being suppressed.

Marla lowered her glasses and looked at Terry, who was
sitting with one leg crossed over the other and her face resting
in her hand. She seemed intrigued, but unsure of where the
sim would go. Marla tuned back in as Val and Grady shared
their first kiss.

The next part of the sim showed Grady and Val getting into a car. Grady drove while Val sat in the front seat, enthralled by something Grady was talking about. Suddenly Val began to get sleepy, and as his eyes closed of their own volition Grady pulled over. Val awoke to a ceiling, and noticed that his arms, legs, and head had all been tied down onto a hard slab. He couldn't move his head to look up but could move it from side to side. The view to his left was a window, and the view on his right looked like a make-shift operation room. He noticed he was connected to an IV drip and saw utensils on a trolley. The walls were wood paneling and felt old. Val rationalized that he must have been in some cabin somewhere. He thought that Grady was taking him to meet his parents.

Val heard Grady walk in but couldn't see him. Val realized how dry his throat was when he tried to speak, and nothing came out. Had he been roofied? Grady spoke before Val could make a second attempt at speaking.

"Did you really think we were in love? That I would ever love someone as impure as you?" Val began to feel pain from the straps binding his wrists and thighs. He turned his head towards the window to relieve some of the pressure on his head.

"There is hope for you, though. You have potential and I think that if you pass all of these tests, if you really prove to me that you're not the horrible person I think you are, maybe, just *maybe*, I can let you go, and we can pick up where we left off. Okay? You'll have to really work hard, though." Val couldn't feel hopeful. Instead, he felt dread.

Over what felt like days but was really minutes, Grady proceeded to rape, torture, and quiz Val. During the day Val was drugged into lucid dreaming, and at night Grady continued his misguided version of trials by ordeal. The only thing Val could really ever see was the moon reflected in the water of a lake outside the window, in varying degrees of motion around the earth.

Eventually, through an unclear stream of events, Val was rescued. Grady was arrested and tried, with Val having to repeat his testimony over and over, take medical and psychological tests to prove that Grady really had lured and tortured him. Val had no family or friends to rely on, just kind G-men and some coworkers who were responsible for Val being reported as missing and ultimately being found. Val couldn't rely on them though—instead he turned to drugs, fentanyl mostly, to numb his pain. He didn't leave his house, opting to sit in the abyss, tearing what was left of his soul apart piece by piece.

Marla was pulled out of her rumination by Terry handing her a Kleenex. As soon as she pulled herself out of the sim, she noticed that tears had streamed down her face. For the first time in about seven years, Marla had cried during a sim. She felt around for the chip she always kept on her, and her suspicions were confirmed.

The sim ended and the nanos in the crim's brain began their work. Marla aggressively wiped away her tears, and Terry blew her nose empathetically. Terry had cried, too, because of what Marla assumed was a terrific story on her part. Marla looked at her watch and saw that it read 3:30, later than she expected. She got up and made a phone call to the crew of people responsible for getting the crim back to jail, who sounded like they weren't keen on getting back to their jobs. Marla was tidying up when Terry's voice broke a silence she hadn't realized was there.

"Is that it?"

"That's it," Marla acknowledged.

"What do we do now?"

"Fill out paperwork. Go home. That's pretty much the job, dude." Marla had finished packing up her supplies and walked towards the door.

"Don't we—I don't even know. I just feel so emotional. That was—that—I don't even know." Then, as Marla had expected, *the* question escaped from Terry's lips. "How do you do something like that to someone and then just, I don't know, go home?"

Marla looked in her bag, and, as if by divine intervention, noticed her carefully sealed envelope, filled with ten years of anger, hatred, depression, and other pent up emotions, and without looking up, she simply said:

"I don't know. I just do."

DVDs

"I'm just saying that I would want my perfect match to own particular pieces of media and that, in relation to that statement, I would want my 'perfect match'—your words, not mine—to have a particular collection of DVDs because *I* believe it says a lot about a person."

"And *I'm* saying you're too particular to have thought that deeply about something so specific."

"You asked me about my perfect match! If they're perfect, then they should have these things. I'm not saying I *wouldn't* date someone who didn't have these DVDs—really what you should be taking away from this is that my ideal partner has the traits that these DVDs belie. I don't know why you're not getting that."

"Whatever."

"You fucking asked, don't judge me. I listened to your whole 'blue eyes, huge tits' thing. Forgive me for having put thought into my partner's personality."

"Look—whatever. Whatever."

"You want to know which DVDs—"

"*Of course* I do. But don't let that go to your head."

"Alright. So, first, but in no particular order, *The Shawshank Redemption* (1994)."

"What even."

Sandy was in the trunk, again, being collected by the dynamic duo, Alex and Ash. They had been sent by Mr. Overstreet to collect Sandy from yet another unsavory predicament. At this time, Sandy was listening to the conversation being had by the two sent to collect him. Sandy groaned, realizing his head was killing him. The trunk was dark and smelled like both marijuana *and* skunk, and though Sandy was accustomed to this trunk, he wouldn't say he was a fan of how it smelled.

"So, when do you buy that DVD? You buy it in a Wal-Mart $7 bin after aimlessly wandering around, you know, and you're like 'I'll just look at the DVDs for a second, I've earned it' because you're walking around Wal-Mart buying things you need like a good adult so you're okay with spending some money on something for yourself, you know, impulsively. So obviously my ideal mate bought *Shawshank* as a little gift to themselves, after adulting."
"That can't be the average experience—"

"How would you know?"
"I just don't think someone would buy it for themselves?"

"Or, you know, they got it as a gift from a well-meaning family member. It's a great movie for falling asleep to but is also, like, a nice film. So, this person, owning this film, probably is just, like, a kind, hopeful person."

Often people didn't like being around him, but he had
deep pockets and loved a good party. You probably know
someone like Sandy; he's the kind of person who always
knows *exactly* how to help someone. He could be fun
when you were just getting to know him, but often he took
people's comfort with him, or at least their unwillingness to
start shit, for granted.

For instance, there was this one time at one of Greer's
clubs when Sandy met this overall nice dude named Arnold
that Helena kept at arm's length but had worked with a
few times. Arnold had really large ears, and what Sandy
didn't know about Arnold was that Arnold's father used to
constantly berate him about his ears.

While Arnold was a functioning adult in society and
could take a minor joke about his ears, for example,
yelling, 'hey, how's it going? Can you *hear* me ok?'
or 'who is this guy, Dumbo?', Sandy took advantage
of what Arnold could handle, not realizing (or
exactly realizing and just thinking he was *right*)
that sometimes it's better to be agreeable instead of witty.

"'Kay. I guess."

"Next, a classic rock concert DVD. My preference is definitely something involving Queen because it means they're probably okay with varying degrees of queerness, which is extremely important to me. Of course."

"Which Queen concert?"

"Queen Live at the Bowl (2004)."

"Solid."

"Oh yeah. This DVD, and any other concert DVD demonstrates that this person likes music to some degree. I mean, Queen is awesome, so it would probably show that they have *good* taste in music, but someone only into classic rock probably does *not* have good taste in music."

"I mean, agree to disagree. Classic rock is awesome."

"Yeah, but you also listen to different kinds of music."

"So?"

"Imagine the kind of person who *only* listens to classic rock."

"Oh, yeah. Okay."

Not only did Sandy make a standard Dumbo comment, he
followed it with "Seriously, you ever thought about plastic
surgery? I know a guy who could take those down about
20%," and then, later, like, too long later in the evening,
Sandy approached Arnold and handed him a card with the
number of a plastic surgeon in New York and, in complete
seriousness, said, "This is Dr. Gregory's card. He's a nice
guy, does great work.

You know, he's done a lot of good work for some ladies
I know who weren't happy with their, er, *natural*
endowments, and I think he could help you."

Well, Arnold kicked his ass right on the spot. The crazy
thing is that Sandy kept trying to defend what he said by
still making comments on Arnold's ears, like, 'yo, I didn't
know you were so sensitive about your ears, man, I just
wanted to help'.

"Yeah. No one under 50 listens to *only* classic rock, and people who listen to *only* classic rock are often, also, the kinds of people who don't really live in the *present*. Nah'mean?"

"Yeah, okay. I get it. Next."

"Well, okay. So, these next ones are important. *Pulp Fiction* (1994) and/or *Jackie Brown* (1997). That's just because I love Tarantino and I think if I'm dating someone around our age, they probably have a copy of *Pulp Fiction* somewhere. And I think if this person has a copy of something by Tarantino, they probably like pop culture and intertextuality, et cetera. It's hard for me to have a conversation without mentioning some piece of pop culture."

"I've noticed."

"So, then you totally understand the Tarantino thing."

"This is starting to feel a lot like a horoscope."

"Do you want me to go through the remaining 16 or not?"

"I absolutely do *not* want to hear the remaining 16, can you give me the Cliff's Notes?"

Arnold was about to bite off one of Sandy's ears when Ash and Alex intervened, told Arnold to call Greer in the morning, and threw Sandy in the trunk.

Sandy ended up in the trunk pretty often, meaning that Alex and Ash had to save him just as frequently. Alex and Ash disliked picking up Sandy but enjoyed being able to throw the boss' shitty son into the trunk of a car.

Certainly, Sandy didn't need to be in the trunk, but Alex and Ash weren't in the mood for his quips. For instance, everyone had gotten together because Greer had hooked up a private screening of the new *Avengers* movie, and it was going to be awesome. Everyone was really excited, and he *talked* the whole time the movie was playing! He was making all these comments, like: 'you know, in the comics, Nebula isn't a robot. Like, the *original* comics'.

"I mean, you're not getting the full image without hearing them all, but I guess I can pick out the important ones."
"Jesus Christ."

"Close, I mean, *The Count of Monte Cristo* with Jim Caviezel (2002). And before you start, I know that's not what you meant. I just thought it was a funny segue."

"What does *owning* this movie say about a person?"
"It says they probably didn't have time to read the book, but they liked the story. I think this is also one of the ones you'd get at Wal-Mart. And it's a great film. It's hard to adapt a 1500-page novel."
"It just says that they're lazy?"
"Practical. It's a classic of course. Everyone knows the story. This person likes to watch it in the background while they cook. It's a good background movie."

'Did you hear that? He said 'I am Groot' but he said it, like, snarky. Like how someone who was making fun of the fact that all he says is 'I am Groot'!' 'I think that I could probably look like Chris Hemsworth if I grew out my hair. I already have the beard and the body'. And before you ask, he definitely did *not* have the body *or* the beard.

Right now, Sandy is in the trunk, listening to the conversation Alex and Ash are having and he is *dying* to contribute. It's sad. Here's some of what he was mumbling in the trunk:

"You know, my ideal partner would probably be someone who goes to the gym, like, five times a week but isn't bulky or anything, mostly she just goes there to stay toned. She would be funny, smart, charming. An awesome cook. She would always be available to chill, like, totally willing to do whatever, whenever. Chill at home or go out. She probably has some dope job at a firm. Somewhere where they do a lot of math, so you know she's book smart and shit. She's an accountant but not one of those accountants that works long hours."

"But what kind of person plays this film in the background?"
"Look who's interested all of a sudden?"
"I just don't think you're digging deep enough."

"Okay, well, it's a movie about a prison break, just like *Shawshank,* except this isn't a TV kind of movie, it's a little more niche. The kind of person who owns this film has probably read the book, but only once. They like classical literature, but in small doses because they just don't have time and they're probably a little snobbish, but I like them a little snobbish."
"Because you're a little snobbish."
"*Ovviamente.*"
"Was that Italian?"
"Yes."

"What's the next one in your Cliff's Notes?"
"A Disney film or two. Probably *the Nightmare before Christmas* (1993), but when it was still just a Touchstone release. It has the best special features."
"Alright."
"Yeah, well, I want my ideal partner to have a sort of childish side. You know? Like, they're someone who needs people because they're a little childish. Maybe that's a DVD they got when they were a kid and they took it with them when they moved out of their parents' place."

Here's the best part:
"Oh, and she would totally let me do her in the butt."
If that doesn't tell you something about Sandy, and
especially how Sandy treats people, let alone women, I'm
not sure what would.

What Sandy didn't know was that Alex and Ash were
actually going to kill him. Unfortunately, step-son or no,
Greer was done with putting up with Sandy. It takes a lot
for a person to want to kill a family member, and it was not
an easy decision for Greer.

"That's... almost romantic."
"Yeah, well, I'm a hopeless romantic."
"I think we have time for one more."

"Well, this is just because they probably got it as a gift. *Slapshot* (1977), or *Creed* (2015) or *Rudy* (1993). A sports movie. Because it shows that they like sports. I don't know, that one is sort of complicated to explain."
"Is it because someone liking sports movies shows that they are into pop culture but probably also played sports, and you want your partner to be athletic?"

It all started to go downhill about three months ago when Sandy got drunk and started harassing some women, one of the women being the wife of one of Greer's colleagues, Simon, who was just trying to have a nice night out with her girlfriends at one of the bars Simon and Greer co-own.

Harassing is a euphemism—he went up behind her when she was dancing and held her until her friends sufficiently distracted him and got her away. He had been trying to hit her up all night, though, that's important to get across, and finally he was drunk enough to try something. Everything devolved from that night; he started getting into coke in a big way, dealing drugs at a university. Now there's a rumor going around that Sandy isn't happy with how Greer is running his mother's empire while she's in the clink (temporarily, fingers crossed!) and wants to kill Greer. Naturally, Greer had to do something. Sandy's behavior had been escalating in the last couple months, but he was always a shithead. He talked a big game about how much he loved his mother, but behind her back would say how even *she* didn't know how to run the various family businesses. Sandy had been talking shit about Greer for years, and even threatened him multiple times. Greer was faced with a difficult decision—kill his step-son and jeopardize his position as interim boss and possibly his life, or let Sandy collect enough names to form a coup and possibly murder him. Greer chose the former.

"Yeah, something like that."

"While we're waiting for the gate to open you want to rattle off some more? You know this thing takes forever."

"Ok. *Thor: Ragnarok* (2016) because it's the best one of the three, *Do the Right Thing* (1989) because Spike Lee is a god of the cinema and it's the kind of movie you don't watch too often because it's so emotionally jarring but you support the artist. *Coffee and Cigarettes* (2003) because it's pretty much my favorite movie of all time—"

"Why do you keep saying the years after all the movies?"

"*Highlander* (1986), *Moonstruck* (1987), because I think my partner should have a sense of humor and both of those films are ridiculous but personal favorites—"

"You basically just want someone who has the same DVD collection as you."

"Not exactly the same..."

"I've seen your DVD collection. You own all of these DVDs as well as two copies of *Live Aid*, *Casablanca*, *Batman: The Animated Series* but only the first two collections, and a whole bunch of other ones that I can't recall right now."

"Why do you know my DVD collection so well?"

"Because I have a great memory. I checked out your collection at that house-warming party you had."

"That's sort of cute."

"Fuck outta here. Anyway. Time to get to work."

"Yep. Next time I'll tell you about what CDs would be best."

"Great."

Sandy felt the car come to a stop. He started to pat around
to make sure he had his phone, wallet, keys, whatnot. Often
the car stopped at this point to allow for the gates to his
mother's home to open, so he was not worried. Suddenly
the trunk popped open and there was a flood of light.
Sandy tried to speak, but Ash stuck a wad of napkins in his
mouth and then sealed his mouth with duct tape while Alex
held a hand against his throat. Alex and Ash stood over
him and said nothing. Sandy went to get out of the trunk,
but again Alex put a hand out to hold him down.

"That's so much better."

Ash pulled out a gun and shot him in the forehead before
Sandy could do or say anything.

Alex and Ash closed the trunk and pushed the car into
the 'natural' pit of sulfuric acid-based 'fertilizer' that had
'formed' in the mountains of Swansea. Luckily, a real-life
Walter White was on the payroll and ensured that the car
and Sandy wouldn't last long in the pit. Alex steered while
Ash pushed. They stripped to their skivvies, threw all their
clothes into the pit along with the car, and changed into the
secondary outfits they left in their other car, parked nearby.
They lit up a joint and watched the car, and any hope they
had of surviving the inevitable shuffling of personnel
after Helena got out of the clink, degrade into high quality
fertilizer.

"Wait, so, you also have a list of CDs?"

The Prince

Once upon a time there was a young prince who ruled a small but prosperous empire.

He was a kind young man, and this kindness extended to his people. He was an empathetic ruler, always trying to do what he could to make his subjects' lives easier. He wasn't gorgeous, or a genius, but he was self-sacrificing, understanding, and good at math.

The Prince ruled over a whole empire, as I said before, making him a very sought-after husband. Princesses came from all over the land to try and grab him as a husband but to no avail. They all tried to use their feminine wiles to entice or seduce him, but none of their tactics worked. Though the princesses didn't know it, they were barking up the wrong tree. The Prince was gay, and unfortunately couldn't act on it due to societal constraints of the time. The Prince, although he wanted to change public perception, was more concerned with making sure the empire was prosperous. Despite that, he couldn't bring himself to marry a woman or, god forbid, sleep with one. This was a source of shame for the Prince—he felt as though the one thing he could do to help his kingdom was form the strongest alliance possible, and he just couldn't bring himself to lie.

Whenever his advisors would implore him to pick a wife and secure his line of succession, he would brush them off; but in a month or so, another woman would be at the palace, trying to seduce him, and the Prince would reject another princess.

"When I find the right woman, I will marry her," he would always say. At the time, the Prince thought there would never be a right woman.

One day, a young princess from a foreign land was brought to the Prince for a meeting. He was uninterested, having a lot of subjects to see that day (who all had a lot of problems), but his advisors implored him, "Aligning ourselves with this family is very important. She brings with her access to a lot of grain and other foods which would really benefit your subjects." The advisors knew just how to get the Prince to listen. The Prince began to formulate a plan in his head, slowly trying to push down the shame welling up inside him. He reluctantly agreed to meet with the woman and her family.

The Prince and his advisors shared a meal with the Princess and her family. Her father was a brash, funny king who aptly ruled over a small neighboring country. The country was quite self-sufficient thanks to a successful alignment with his wife, the Queen's, kingdom. She was an intelligent lady with peering eyes and a serious face. The Princess, though reserved, was lovely and had the same peering eyes as her mother.

After eating, the advisors, King, and Queen sojourned into the adjacent drawing room so the Prince and Princess could become better acquainted. They sat and smoked while the Queen told exceptional, interwoven stories that left all listeners enthralled.

The Prince had a whole speech prepared for the Princess, meant to let her down easily but still leaving an open-ended conclusion such that the two of them could come to a reasonable agreement about how to best govern their kingdoms together.

He opened his mouth to speak, but the Princess beat him to it, falling on her knees and sobbing, "Oh, Prince! Please, please help me. Everyone says you are a kind ruler who always does what's best for his people—does this extend to me? To someone like me?" The Prince was interested out of concern and curiosity and bade the woman to continue.

"I fell in love with one of my father's guards. We grew up together—him, the son of one of my father's generals, and me, the Princess. We were educated together, we would play together, we were as close as could be. Everything was so easy when we were young." She sobbed a little, took a deep breath, and continued in a wavering tone.

"We knew that one day I would be promised to someone else and that he would be asked to go to war. We didn't know which would come first. We hoped that he would distinguish himself enough in a war to-to-to—" the Prince handed her a handkerchief and patted her shoulder. She took another deep breath.

"We hoped he would prove himself to my father and that maybe we could get married. We were so hopeful. The night before he was set to leave for a battle, we laid together and promised ourselves to one another. We were so in love." She paused and sighed, having regained some of her usual composure. "A month later, he died honorably on the battlefield. I couldn't even cry at his funeral because I just couldn't believe it. No one knew of our love and, like that, it was over.

"I knew that my only duty after his death, then, was to my country. I resolved to marry whomever I had to to help my people. That's what he would have wanted. I cried for weeks in the privacy of my room, but outwardly, I was the picture of diplomacy. I sat by my father's side to learn how to rule the kingdom, I studied the histories and philosophers, and I met with the people. But a month after his death—two months after we had laid together—I still had not bled."

The Prince furrowed his brow and unconsciously looked at her belly. Now that she was sitting, he could almost see the faint outline of her stomach from beneath her robes. At first, he thought the flowing nature of her gown was an attempt at modesty, but now realized it was strategy on her part. The Prince inhaled deeply.

"How long has it been?" he asked sternly.

"Four months. Four months and I feel a child inside of me. I love this child more than I ever loved its father, but what am I to do? The other Princes my father introduced me to, they would never have believed that he was their child. I don't want my child to be resented or questioned or disrespected by a man who is unable to love a child that is not theirs." She spoke strongly, but the Prince noticed her digging her nails into her palm.

"A month or two ago, it was more possible. Who would believe me now? What man would believe me five months from now when I give birth to a fully-formed child?" Tears rolled down her cheeks, but she would not open her mouth again, seemingly afraid of what sounds may come out. The Prince helped her off her knees and onto the sofa beside him.

The Prince took her hands in his and smiled softly, "I have never said this to anyone before, Princess, but because I think we can both help each other, and I want you to know my motivations, I'll tell you this. I have no desire to lay with a woman, and I will never desire to lay with a woman. What I really, truly want," he paused, "is to lay with another man." The Princess nodded slowly at first. Then, her head shot up.

"Then, you'll marry me? I promise I will never, *ever* make you lay with me. I promise to share all my books with you, and we can be great friends. We can raise this child together," she smiled and put her hands on her belly, "and in this way, he will know true love."

The two people, brought together by coincidence, announced their betrothal that evening and were married two days later.

As someone once said, on a long enough timeline, the survival rate for everyone drops to zero. Although the Prince, Princess, and their son spent a decade living in prosperity, fate had other plans for them, which started with a magician named Simonides and the foreign King he served.

Simonides was the court magician for the King, and he had many different powers. He could conjure, and change, and create, but he was best known for his ability to see. Simonides could see into the future (if he tried), and this was why the King had risen to such prosperity, and why Simonides had been able to live as long as he had. One night, as Simonides was attempting to look into the future, he saw our Prince sitting on a golden throne and looking over an empire on fire. Simonides' King was kneeling on the floor in front of the Prince while Simonides was bound by some guards. The Prince stood up and drew his sword. As he swung it high into the air, Simonides cried out and the King's head was lobbed clean off. It rolled to Simonides' feet.

Simonides ran to the King's bedroom and told him about the vision. Almost immediately the two began formulating a plan to stop the Prince before he could cause any damage. Simonides recognized how the Prince was dressed, and using his spy network as a resource, deciphered which Prince and which country would try to destroy them. The King gathered his troops and began to march.

The Prince heard through his advisors about the oncoming attack. He was admittedly scared. He wanted to protect his people, his wife, and his son, but didn't know how. Everyone gave him advice.

The generals said, "We must meet this king on the battlefield. Our army is small but strong. We can kill this king, take his land, and become more prosperous because of it."

The Prince did not want to do this, because it was likely to result in more death.

The advisors said, "We must use diplomacy. This King has a daughter—we must give your son to him in exchange for peace and broker a marriage deal that will protect your people."

The Prince did not want to do this because he did not want to sacrifice his son to this King, an exchange that may or may not work.

The people screamed, "We all must run away, for this King is ruthless."

The Prince knew running and hiding was impossible for him, though he wished his people who did so all the best.

The Princess said, "You must surrender. You must do whatever it takes to convince this King you do not want his kingdom. The advisors should organize a meeting with him, and there you can prostrate yourself before him and beg him for mercy. We cannot hope to survive otherwise."

The Prince did the math on the probability of a successful outcome, and he rationalized that the Princess was right. This tactic would put him in danger, but it was the only course with a likely positive outcome. He had heard rumors about this king being ruthless but had also heard about him being just. The Prince was banking on the latter.

The Prince convinced his advisors to organize a meeting between himself and the King. They tried to change his mind, but it was impossible. At dawn, two days later, the Prince walked into the King's camp.

The Prince walked into the King's tent and immediately got on his knees. "Oh, King. I have never had any malintent towards you, and I wish to do whatever it takes to resolve this problem to protect my people and my family. Ask anything of me and anything I shall give." The Prince would not lift his head to look at the King.

The King and Simonides were both baffled. This was the ruthless ruler Simonides had seen in his vision? They looked at each other, and Simonides shrugged.

"Ottoman Prince, stand up," the King said, walking towards the Prince. "I do not want to start a war with you—" suddenly, yells rose from outside the tent. The Prince's generals had launched an attack in secret.

Rage began to boil in the King. He ran out of his tent and told his soldiers to fight off the small army with no restraint. He ran around, rousing men from their tents and helping with armor until he remembered the Prince of these callous soldiers was in his tent. The King stalked back to the Prince.

The King grabbed the Prince by the hair and lifted his head up. They looked each other in the eye, and the King, a seasoned warrior, saw fear in the Prince's eyes. But the King knew a man could be afraid and at the same time be the organizer of a coup. He let go of the Prince's hair and let his head drop.

"You disgust me." The King spat. He drew his sword and used it to balance, crouching before the Prince. "Everyone describes you as kind, and empathetic, and reserved. Never have they described you as deserving of respect." The King regained his composure temporarily. "Your soldiers knew this was the tactic you would take, and yet they did not respect your decision. Will they respect you in death, do you think?" The Prince hung his head, knowing that the answer was no.

"I only ask that whatever you do to me, you leave my wife and son be. They had nothing to do with this. I ask for mercy on them, ruler to ruler—" The King scoffed aloud.

"After I hold your severed head for all to see, you will be no ruler. But I will show them mercy. More mercy than your men showed mine." And with that, the King lobbed off our Prince's head.

After the King rode out holding the Prince's head, the battle died down. The generals and troops were no match for an army as large as the King's. The King walked into the palace and found the Princess and her son had gone. He had no desire to chase them.

Simonides, while the King was out quelling the battle, turned the still crouched body of the Prince into stone, and after the battle had it brought to the throne room. The King used the body of the Prince to rest his feet, and eventually the stone looked less and less like a body and more like nothing but a rock.

And that is where ottomans come from.

Twenty-Three Different Jobs

"You start *in medias* res, you know—you always start in medias res, unless you're J.K. Rowling or something. She wrote—of course you know who J.K. Rowling is! Everyone fucking knows who J.K. Rowling is," sighed Sam, our protagonist, never more focused in his life. Though he had walked away for a second, he made his way back to the desk, and again pointed the gun at Harvey.

"So," he began, "I've spent all this time writing, sending out manuscripts—a bunch of them to you *Harv*—and nothing. Nothing has happened. I'm tired of getting nowhere. I've had twenty-three different jobs in the last five years to... to gain perspective!" Sam rubbed his thumb and forefinger together obsessively, trying to pull thoughts together before losing his train of thought. "I've got a manuscript now—the other ones, you know, maybe they weren't so good—obviously you didn't think so, *Harvey*," Sam spat his name and even someone as generally uncaring as Harvey was disgruntled by his name being treated like a curse word. "This one, Harvey," Sam put the gun to his own head and made a clicking motion while exhaling, using his other hand to indicate brains spilling out;

the universal symbol for a mind being blown. "This one is just—wow—so much better. I'm reluctant to give this to you though, Harvey. You gave up on the other ones so quickly and you might just want to *bandwagon* onto my success with this one because it's so good. But, I gotta earn a living somehow, so I'll let you make some money off me if it means finally getting published." Sam stopped short, realizing he was pacing, and not paying attention to his hostage.

Sam sauntered over to Harvey's desk and sat opposite him in a chair that was purely for aesthetics. He lazily handled the gun, something that obviously made Harvey uncomfortable. "I've dreamt of this moment, Harvey," Sam said softly, genuinely, he would later note. He had legitimately wanted to meet Harvey for years—this was the man who had discovered Stephen King when he was still writing shorts at U of Maine, which Sam had overheard Harvey say at an event they had both attended, Sam as a server and Harvey as Harvey.

"This is... I'm pretty sure the first time we're in the same room together, Harv, buddy," Sam remarked, looking out the window behind Harvey's desk but keeping an eye on him. "Well, sort of. I've served at events you've been at, dropped off manuscripts and stuff, but we've never actually exchanged words. You never actually read any of my manuscripts, did you?" Sam's temperament changed as the painful truth dawned on him; Harvey's micro reactions indicated as much. Harvey opened his mouth to speak but Sam interrupted, shrugging nonchalantly, with such malice that even someone as smarmy as Harvey shut his mouth. "No matter, Harvey. I knew you never read my 'scripts. I'm not a big name and you only publish big names here." Sam got up from the desk and looked at all the books on Harvey's wall shelves. Mostly copies of classics and Stephen King novels. Sam rolled his eyes to himself, thinking *Harvey didn't even sign King*, and when he turned around, Harvey was resting his face in his hand, covering his mouth as if to hide it. This unsettled the typically settled Sam, though he couldn't understand why.

Harvey, who had a deep-seated fear of death and frequently attempted to be the most pragmatic man in the room, had installed a panic button under his desk, right where his hidden hand was, just a week ago—after weeks of incessant calling by his secretary (at Harvey's request) to the panic-button company (literally called Panic Buttons for You). This panic button activated a switch on his secretary's phone which would cause a light to flash on Arthur's desk that advised him to call the police promptly. Arthur, he supposed, would see the light sometime in the next twenty minutes, so Harvey decided to use his time wisely, namely, to discover more about Sam and keep him talking. He believed this a wise choice based on television shows he had ingested as a child and continued to enjoy in his adulthood.

"Tell me about these twenty-three jobs you've had. I mean, what kind of jobs were they?" Harvey was starting to get up, but this was not what Sam wanted.

Sam pointed the gun more directly at Harvey, and barked, "What do you think you're doing?" a threat framed as a question.

Harvey put his hands up in surrender, admitting, "I was just going to grab a glass of water. Do you want anything? Bar's fully stocked." Harvey continued to get up, slowly, and Sam pointed the gun less intensely, more out of habit. Harvey felt his hands steady and the knot in his chest loosen slightly.

Sam studied Harvey, his security guard training taking over. Harvey seemed to be motivated by self-preservation, not only in his movements but in his willingness to listen. "I like you, Harvey. Every time we've been in the same room together and I've heard you tell stories; it's felt as though you were an honest person—nothing superfluous about you. Even your outfit today screams practicality," Harvey was wearing brown slacks and a pale blue dress shirt, no tie; he liked this outfit for no reason other than it was comfortable in comparison to his usual suits and ties. "You seem to have no interest in playing the hero, Harvey." Harvey chuckled as he poured water from a simple decanter into a simple glass, contemplating this odd compliment.

"It's nice to hear you say that, Sam." Harvey moseyed to his desk and sat down. He had poured Sam a glass of water.

"And, well, if I'm being honest, being a hero never got me anywhere. I never hard-core fucked anyone over, but I never really went out of my way for anyone for the sake of doing so. If I'm considered a champion of the people while making myself a lot of money, so be it, but I've never actively strove to construct a hero-type narrative for myself." Harvey took a sip of water and opened his arms wide to draw attention to his office and all the stuff in it, "I didn't design this office, and truth be told I only use about ten percent of it. All this stuff is in here because my daughter, a designer, told me that having all these material things would demonstrate a certain degree of power to whoever came into this office. Do you feel this office indicates that I have power, Sam?"

Sam looked around and scoffed involuntarily. He felt compelled to explain himself. "I can see why someone would think that you're powerful based on all the stuff, but based on the lack of fingerprints on mostly everything—and I know you have an oily, mostly-Italian diet so there would be fingerprints, in addition to the fact that I know you don't allow anyone to clean this office, I mean, you even take the garbage out yourself—I can tell that you don't really care for it. But you were saying," Sam said, proud of himself.

Harvey nodded. "I guess you were a detective at some point, too?"

"No, I just read a lot of Conan Doyle."

"Ah, well. Me, too. As a child. I also watched a lot of Hitchcock's films. Anyway, all of this is mine. I spent a lot of money on this office that I barely use, and I can afford to pay for it because I built this company on the backs of writers like you. Whether they were famous before I got to them or I made them famous through sheer force of will is always up for debate." Harvey turned to look out of his large window and absently rubbed his thumb and index finger together. "When I was starting out, I tried a little more to seem like a hero, but now—well, you know how it is, Sam." Some people called Harvey 'El Diavolo' because making a deal with him was like making a deal with the devil—you would receive what you wanted, but at a price, and you never knew the price until it was too late. This is important information for you to note.

"So, Sam, give me a little context. The police are probably on their way, as well as the press. Tell me about this manuscript and then let's try and make a deal. We don't have a lot of time," Harvey finished his water and got up to grab an actual drink, choosing a bottle of whiskey and gesturing to Sam with it, silently offering. Sam nodded, pursing his lips.

Though you don't know too much about Sam at this point, you must know that he isn't the awkward loner type that would usually do this sort of thing in movies or television programs. Sam is an intellectual, but aware of social ques and conventions. He got twenty-three different jobs in the difficult economy of 2010s North America, and chose them methodically, never struggling to make rent in his downtown loft. He is charming, interesting—borderline sociopathic in the opinion of his last three partners—and, ultimately, a businessman. He immediately understood what Harvey was doing and was impressed.

"First, I got a job at a family-run B&B and worked as a secretary-slash-caretaker for the family, because the parents didn't want to work at the place anymore, and I wrote about that and some of the real oddballs I met working there.

"Next I worked at a used car dealership and wrote a piece of short fiction about a day in the life of Matilda's dad, you know, from the Roald Dahl book—"

"That'll be a tough one to publish because of copywriting. You might need to edit it to be a more general character."

"I also wrote about having Douglas Coupland as a family friend."

"Better. Keep going."

Sam sat down and crossed one leg over the other, settling comfortably into the crux of his well-worn pitch. "I guess I wanted to create a collection of short pieces that are indicative of the real human experience but sort of askew and subversive. I got a job as a janitor in a big hospital in the city and wrote a listicle about the eight things you wouldn't expect to find in a hospital garbage as frequently as you do. Then there was the grave-digger job which lent itself to a short story about a piece of jewelry that gets passed from generation to generation. Then I lied and got a job as an electrician without any training, so I wrote about how easy it is to lie about that sort of thing—"

"An exposé type thing—"

"Exactly. I was a pimp for a little while and I wrote a short piece of fiction about an undercover agent-slash-hooker who got embroiled in a body-disposal plot with a fellow sex worker. I was a computer cleaner—like people's actual files— and wrote about file names for stuff you don't want people to find. Like, if you had a bunch of bestiality porn on your computer what would be the best name for that file folder to hide it from someone who might see your files. Not really a story, *per se*—I just really like to experiment with *form*, you know? I was a flight attendant for two weeks and I wrote a piece about how difficult it is to join the Mile-High Club on commercial flights. I wrote a couple of faux news articles, some really experimental pieces, and after that I was a bouncer at a—"

Before Sam could say anything more, someone stronger than him grabbed him and pulled him out of the chair. He watched as Harvey grabbed the manuscript and put it in his desk drawer, all in slow motion, and as Sam's head crashed into the floor and the wind left his chest in a hurry, his vision began to fail.

Acknowledgements

I'm going to try to not be that writer that thanks more people in their acknowledgements than they have pages in their book, but no promises.

Thank you to my Mom. My Beverly Goldberg. I love you, thank you for being the only person I know I can count on. You're my hero and my stylist. I'm grateful to know you'll always support me, and I hope I'm as strong as you when I finally grow up. Thank you for encouraging me and keeping me close. You've lived life with *and* without me, and you still choose to keep me in it. I love you.

To my biological and chosen dads, who have both had the pleasure of being married to my mom and living with me. Thank you for always helping me with projects and carrying the heavy boxes for me. And other stuff, like, you know, listening to me, being there for me, and showing me cool music and TV shows, shows that would later influence the writing in this very book. Thank you.

Thank you to my friends, especially all the ones who like me. Thank you for listening to me rant and more (i.e., Cor, Daniela, Sil, Deeds), and making me feel like I'm not the only person who likes certain things (i.e., LeiLei, James McQuay, Ayleen Schokking, John Lawler, Eva Baglieri, Ashley Romano), for liking me even though we're family (i.e., Lucas, Dano, Zia x2, Zio x2, May, Alex, Casey), and for liking me even though we're not (Kym, David x2, Eddy, Xander, Monica Guignard, James Gutenberg.), and for listening to me bounce good and bad ideas with you (i.e., James Papoutsis, Jenise Lee, Gabriel Broderick, Esq.). Additionally, thank you to everyone who heard me talk about this book, who let me tell them about some of my stories, or who met me this year (for the first of third time)—you people probably contributed more than you think.

Thank you to Gord Downie and The Tragically Hip, Douglas Coupland, Joni Mitchell, Alanis Morisette, Queen Street West, Humbaba's, and all my other favorite Canadian things. Maple Syrup. Root's *men's* salt and pepper elastic ankle sweatpants, poutine. All those weird kid's shows, Algonquin Park, the Humber River Trail. Multicultural cities and small towns. I'm sorry most of these are based in Toronto but flying across Canada is too expensive. Canada and North America in general would not exist without the Indigenous tribes who were here before us immigrants. For the place I grew up, those tribes are the Ashinawabewaki and Huron-Wendat. Thank you, merci.

I wish I could find better ways to thank editors and, specifically, editors who published me. Simply, thank you to Founders College, Women in Higher Education, and Trash Magazine, for not only publishing me, but for having wonderful editors who helped turn good works into great works. Kimmy, I told you I'd write something nice about you here! You rock, and I'm so grateful that I met a kindred spirit in you. Thanks for editing this whole thing and making it into something better than it was. Hopefully the world brings us together a second time in the real world. Thank you, thank you, thank you.

Thank you to every female author that made my publication of this book possible. If I had been born at a different time, or even born now but in other place (by pure happenstance), I might not have had this opportunity. I am grateful to the women who make my life possible every day by fighting for rights I didn't even know I enjoyed. We have a long way to go, and I will continue to do my small part to bring women's rights to the forefront and use my influence for good. Thank you.

Lastly, to the love of my life. It would be almost *impossible* for you to break up with me now, I'm a published author.

And I guess you gotta write a book now, huh?

About the Author

The author is a writer, designer, poet, and amateur artist based out of Toronto, Ontario. She graduated York University for an honors bachelors in History and English in 2018, and is putting her degree to good use by creating often and for free. Among her many hobbies, she enjoys critically examining historical films and critiquing them for historical inaccuracies, correcting people's grammar and citing her English degree, and spending time with people who don't mind either of those hobbies.

Printed in the United States
By Bookmasters